Other Bella Books by Lyn Dowland

Distance Learning

Acknowledgment

With huge thanks to Bella Books for making this possible, and to my editor, Vicki, for a valuable master class.

About the Author

Lyn Dowland is a widely traveled working musician living in the United Kingdom. In addition to poems and plays, she has always written for personal pleasure.

KETTLE'S SPOUT
1500

THE CALF
2200

DANGER
CLIFFS

RUINS

SHEEP TRACK

INN

WINDER
1551

CHURCH

REDBRIDGE'S

ARTS MILL
× Gill

× BAKERY

BLACKFORD

HELTON
FARM

Further Information

Blackford is based on Sedbergh in the Howgill Fells.

Kettle's Spout is Cautley Spout at Cautley Crag, below The Calf.

Many of the points of reference, Winder, the Arts Mill (Farfield), secondhand bookshops, Temperance Inn (Cross Keys) and bakery can all be found, but all characters are fictitious.

Some fictional liberties have been taken with the titles and geographical locations of the golf club, pubs, church, Helton and Meadow Farms and Redbridge's practice.

Sandi's private bathing locations will remain private (and fictional).

There really are ancient ruins of a settlement below Cautley Crag, although the legend itself is purely imaginative, but who knows what actually may have happened there?

Dedication

Joan, L and others who had to find their own
Winder Path.

CHAPTER ONE

Blackford—where the path begins

When Gillian Pembury squeezed her car into the last remaining space of a small car park behind the austere building that housed Redbridge Veterinary Practice, she was certain that she had arrived at the end of the line. Single was how she was arriving and single was how she would remain in a place this small and isolated. Her mood drooped with the last remnants of the old autumn leaves. Late winter was not the most naturally hospitable time to be arriving.

Still, she had promised herself she would focus on her work. She tidied her appearance, scrutinizing herself in the rearview mirror. So far other relationships, even the presence of attractive females, had served only to decimate her concentration levels and obstruct her professional ambitions. At least that was what she was currently telling herself. It helped to convince her that she could, perhaps *should*, manage on her own without her thoughts wandering annoyingly out of her control. Anyway, it would just be for a few years, until she worked out where to head off to next. Perhaps being here was a deliberate attempt to keep herself out of the way of distractions. She stepped lightly out of the car, the bite of the still seasonally cold air catching her by surprise, as she made a concerted effort to sweep away the mental autumn leaves. Time just to be left alone for a while. She was unable to go as far as admitting that perhaps she was running away.

She unloaded some of her bags and headed into the surgery, applying herself to the task of moving some of her work equipment into her locker. She made an insignificant-looking figure: petite, dark hair cut into a tidy, practical bob, humbled against the backdrop of the Howgill Fells. Anyone looking down towards the village from up there would have failed to see her, not even comparable to a mite on an ant on a speck of grit from that majestic distance.

From somewhere inside the depths of the building a healthy voice—Bridget's voice— called a welcome, "Gillian? Is that you?"

Work and progress had been her preoccupation recently. She had landed this countryside position soon after two years of breaking herself in at an intense urban practice in York in the north of England. The mostly small animal work was busy and repetitive, where she was often treated as the dogsbody. When the opportunity had arisen to apply for a vacancy out of the city in a broader, large-animal district, she had thrown herself eagerly into preparation for the interview.

Bridget Redbridge, the established, robust owner of the practice, now approaching her mid-forties Gill guessed, had been impressed with her enthusiasm and the encouraging references. Gill had sat patiently during her interview while Bridget ploughed through her CV, reading aloud about her year in Africa after graduation. Even if it did not directly apply to working in Yorkshire, what an adventurous undertaking, showing strength of character to tackle those difficult situations and stubborn, weighty beasts, and how that would be of use with the farmers. Bridget had exclaimed this with some mirth, apparently delighted by her ingenious comparison. The assessment continued to blossom, Bridget commenting on how Gill's upbringing on the edge of rural Herefordshire would evidently give Gill some instinctive empathy. When she had been invited down for a trial week at the Redbridge practice, continuing compliments on her easy manner with the animals and determination to reach the diagnosis appeared to be the deal-clinchers.

Subsequently, after all the furor of succeeding, it wasn't until Gill had arrived and moved into her little rented house by the old mill buildings of Blackford, crunching over the thin layer of ice on the puddles, that the possible consequences of her removal from any sort of social life began to dawn on her. 'National Park Centre'. It was not that the village lacked promise. Blackford was nestled into a picturesque valley-bowl of the Dales, sizeable enough to house a post office, a school, a sprinkling of shops including a compact village supermarket, an independent delicatessen grocery and some cottage industries, such as the local cheese factory and crafts, all of which enticed the tourists. In the height of the summer the place was buzzing, while still being remote enough to attract committed hikers, cavers and climbers.

The old mill building had been renovated into an arts center and it had a background buzz of new ideas and initiatives rubbing up against traditions. She was close enough to cycle to the practice if she didn't need to go further afield, and the roar of the Mill Race River outside the cottage pleasantly obliterated the world beyond. Perched on the crazy-paved back patio she could watch for dippers or wagtails foraging in the river and even the occasional mink or otter, while thoughtfully sipping a drink, putting her world into better perspective. Her neighbors on either side were kind enough. One kept Jack Russell terriers, the other poodles. Who would even question them for wanting dogs in this area? The walking country was fabulous, the hills beckoning just half a mile away, sometimes dusted with snow, a gorgeous backdrop. No wonder the artists were springing up around there, Gill had mused to herself.

Faced with the prospect of unpacking more boxes, she had decided to explore the arts center instead. The renovation of the old mill warehouse had included preserving some of its old textile looms along with an historical guided walk, which she decided to save for later, preferring to browse the original embroideries, pottery, pictures and craft items in the warmth of the mill shop. Individual artists' studios crowded around the edges of the central display area. She was particularly taken with some appliqué pictures made from remnants of materials interwoven with well-chosen threads to create brightly colored landscapes and rushing rivers. At the organic café in the basement, which would certainly become a useful emergency watering hole, she stirred her coffee, mulling over her thoughts.

It was what she had intended, she told herself. Independence, a degree of self-imposed isolation.

Bridget was capable, reasonably jovial, and showed all the signs of being a fair and dependable boss. Happily married to an accountant, she was an intelligent, experienced colleague who was generous with her time and wages and was equally glad to share a drink at the end of the day. She had already demonstrated these qualities during Gill's trial week.

After a month staying at a comfortable guesthouse in the village, even though the landlady had overflowed with hospitality, Gill's move to the mill cottage had made her glad to have her privacy back. The first few back-breaking weeks of heavy-duty large animal practice in freezing outbuildings had made it feel necessary to step away from the village at the end of the day, into her own private reverie at the mill cottage. Chortling comments from weathered farmers at the arrival of this relatively petite, demure youngish thing from 'down south' wore thin on occasion. Gill had managed to wrong-foot several of them with her tales of charging bull elephants, angry hippos, raging lions and malaria as she injected, stitched and healed their herds.

She had started to add to the talk of the village, without realizing it. There had been an invitation to look in at the Women's Institute meeting, but as yet there had not been a moment to head off to any larger metropolis. And strangely, she was beginning not to mind. It was perhaps the absorption with her work, the lack of opportunity to become distracted that she had been seeking. Even if somewhere inside herself, vaguely she was aware of some unfulfilled dichotomy and that perhaps tumbleweed was blowing across the road of her social life.

Anyway, there was some intimacy of a different kind in a place this compact. The small high street was crammed with useful shops. Already she was recognized at the bakery, the news agency and the secondhand bookshops. A trip to the tiny, independent cinema had been like stepping into a private club. She had sunk into the well-used, padded upholstery of the faded seats and been immersed in the whole experience more closely than at the massive multiplex in York.

In a village the size of Blackford there was space to breathe, just, but still the reassurance that people were looking out for you. She wondered whether that would gradually become people intruding into your business and claustrophobia. She smiled to herself. Only time would tell.

CHAPTER TWO

The meeting of two paths

About six weeks into the new job, on a Friday night at one of the local pubs, The Hounds, Gill was happily ensconced in a settle by the roaring fire with Bridget, her husband Alan, the other assistant vet Ethan and two of the practice nurses, Mandy and Becka, when a small group of local farmers thudded into the bar, steam rising from the hubbub of their voices as they brought the cold night air in from the porch. The end of week socials were a welcome outlet for everyone Gill thought as she looked up to watch and assess the group's arrival, startled by the noise, reaching for her beer to cover herself.

"Take no notice of that intimidating lot. Their bark's worse than their bite." Alan grinned. "It's just the end of the monthly meeting of the local Farmer's Association. It usually gets a bit raucous."

She recognized several from her work rounds already. Some were strangers. All were male. Wives had been left at home. Or so she thought until she noticed a tall figure at the back that turned to join the group after hanging her coat on the pub's coat stand.

Gill was immediately struck by her. The stranger was tall and athletic in build, with an open-necked shirt, her hair pulled into a rough bunch at the back, exposing the angles of cheekbones and a slightly masculine muscular jawline, just on the female side of androgynous about the face, but also shapely about the figure. She stood out from the group, not just because she was the only woman, but by standing an inch or two above some of the men. She headed to the bar counter, leaning comfortably on it with one arm, while pointing across to her choice of pump, laughing with Lucy, the barmaid. The engaging face was lit up by a generous smile.

Gill caught herself analyzing the stranger and nudged her neighbor, Mandy. "Who's that? She's a bit courageous to be the only female, isn't she?"

"Hah! You could say! If it were anybody else. That's Sandi Helton. She owns Helton Farm with her brother John. He's the one in the corner with the green fleece jacket."

"Oh." Gill let her eyes wander to take in the brother. There was a noticeable family resemblance in the aquiline nose, although the brother was darker both in complexion and hair color and seemed to be caught up animatedly in a serious discussion.

"Gill, what do you think?" Bridget called for her attention.

"Ugh? Sorry?"

"About converting the outhouses into something more useful? Alan says kennels, Ethan suggests recovery rooms. Maybe a dispensary?"

"How about a little of everything? Kennels would prove useful. Maybe we could provide an occasional holiday kennel service for absent owners, some additional income, with a larger recovery area for the practice and a back-up dispensary? As long as it's all secure?"

Gill's attention was pulled back to the discussion and time passed before there was a moment to look away without seeming impolite. Then it was her turn to get a round in.

She gathered up the glasses and headed to the bar. While she waited for service she watched the farmers. Some had settled into groups at small tables, several still leant against the counter. She scanned them for another glimpse of the imposing Sandi, now apparently elusive and not to be seen. One of the more familiar stockholders raised a hand in greeting to her. *Well, perhaps she's headed home.* A nudge at her elbow from her other side broke the reverie and Gill jumped as she realized the figure pushing a glass forward next to her through a press of people was the one she had been seeking out.

"Oops, sorry." The tall woman apologized.

"Oh, no worries."

"Australian are we?"

"Er…no."

She grinned. "Hi, I'm Sandi." She reached over a work-roughened hand.

"Oh, hi. Gill."

"Yes, I know. The new vet. Frank said you were a dreamboat with his new Hereford."

"That's kind of him."

"Well, they weren't his exact words…more like 'she dun a greet job with mee new bull'."

"Ah…" Further conversation was postponed by the interruption of Lucy taking a drinks order and chiming in with her own running commentary on the cheekiness of the local farmers and the general hubbub in the pub, even for a Friday night. Sandi raised her glass to Gill in a gesture of finality and turned to talk to her neighbor, leaving Gill with the uncomfortable feeling that she was sorry there was no more to say.

She returned to her table. The conversation had reverted to relaying funny stories from the week and gradually metamorphosed into sporting events over the weekend. Becka tried to persuade Gill to join the local girls for netball or football sometimes and it was as she was signaling 'No way' with her hands that she noticed Sandi grinning at her from the bar. Gill raised her eyebrows in surprise and looked away quickly. She found herself unable to look that way again, suddenly self-conscious. Something prickled across the back of her neck and out onto her shoulders, like a heat rash. She threw herself back into the immediate conversation, trying to distract herself.

It was not until she headed for the ladies' that she saw the tall, willowy girl again. Sandi was coming out, back into the bar, as Gill was approaching down the same narrow corridor. They stopped, faced with the predicament of passing each other.

"Hi, again."

"Excuse me." They said simultaneously and laughed. Without reversing there was nowhere to go apart from squeezing through, which was the best option, so they did precisely that. As their hips brushed each other Gill risked a glance up to the other woman, only to find herself looking into warm, kind brown eyes and a smiling mouth that revealed healthy white teeth, all surrounded by very touchable-looking skin. It was a momentary glance that assessed so much in just a split second. They both stopped. Struck by an inexplicable sense of something significant.

"Busy tonight, isn't it?" Gill offered.

"And a bit of a squeeze…" Sandi chuckled.

Then they moved on.

"See you!" Gill murmured.

From the retreating figure she could have sworn that she heard: "Hope so."

A smile crossed her lips. She told herself off for the faint stirrings that crossed her body.

That night, tucked up at her cottage, Gill was bugged by the repeating images of the woman, Sandi. She was annoyed and slightly intrigued. Annoyed to find her thoughts straying distractedly, but the annoyance wasn't winning. Something inside her was curious, requesting the option of another chance encounter.

CHAPTER THREE

The Heart of the Dales

"*It is not infrequently the dampest of places and quite often one of the most beautiful of places in England.* Ha! Look at this!" Becka was reading from a magazine article, while they kicked back for a moment with a pot of coffee in the surgery kitchen. She leant on the counter, leafing through the pages, as Gill poured out four coffees to suit their owners.

"No bloody kidding," she continued. "You haven't been up on the moors in the depths of winter yet have you, Gill?"

"Nope. But I'm looking forward to it."

"Er, I wouldn't look too forward to it. You can die from it."

Gill cast her mind back a few days. She had been tempted to drive past Helton Farm, slightly curious after the comments that were made at the pub. After a short trip out of the village, she found it, about a third of the way up the hillside, where the pastures were still green and moist, before the harshness of the moorland climate could overpower the photosynthetic ability of the plants, a compact, determined smallholding, Helton Farm, clinging to the slopes. It seemed to be home to some of the hardiest breed of Swaledale sheep, a small but thriving shorthorn cattle herd and, so she had heard, an almost equally robust brother and sister. The remote buildings still part of the outlying edges of the rural community, balancing along the hilltops symptomatic of the backbone of England, still picturesque and autonomous despite the best efforts of the outside world to force changes upon it, she mused.

"Yorkshire. Renowned in Britain for its teabags, cheese, sheep farming, walking country and a history of textile industries. Also well-known for its stubbornly determined folk and stunning scenery." Becka's voice chimed in.

Gill still chuckled when her route took her along the M62 motorway's opposing carriageways, where they are forcibly separated, like a pair of fire irons, by a farm at Windy Hill purportedly because the owner was of the doggedly stubborn type who refused to sell up. Myth or legend perhaps, or maybe just rock strata, but it goes to show that's how stubborn Yorkshire folk are reputed to be—that roads are forced to go around the ragged hills, steep valleys and determined countryfolk.

She smiled as she sugared two of the coffees, drawn back to Becka by her readings.

"Harsh winters encroach upon the valleys, making mountains of hay and cozy barns necessities for the animals. Even in the warmer seasons, sudden rain showers, as quick to depart as they are to arrive, cause the surrounding hills to weep waterfalls that form crystal clear streams, plummeting down the hillsides, maturing into winding brooks with pebbled beaches, then lazier gravy-colored, peat water rivers, framed forever by the rolling hills, the crumpled bedspread of the bleak moorland tops where their journeys began. A magical land of limestone caves and steep valleys, where iron-age villages had clustered once at the bottom of waterfalls, superstitiously fascinated by the unending sources of pouring, life-giving water." Becka continued, really sinking into her role as self-appointed tour guide.

"It is in the lush valleys, the sometimes boggy, sometimes meadow-filled lowlands that the biscuit-tin villages and small towns nestle in now, laid out in interlocking grey stone, the jigsaws of drystone walls spreading out arterially from their boundaries. Those communities

*carve their livings through their usual daily needs and the trading,
farming, tourism and local industry definitive to the area.* There
you are Gill. That's what you needed—a beginner's guide to
Yorkshire." She giggled and gave Gill a friendly squeeze around
the shoulders.

"Thanks a lot. Now drink your coffee."

While Becka continued chatting, Gill's thoughts drifted.
She wondered…at Helton, were they averse to the advances of
the modern world. Or did they spend the evening immersed
online to avoid the fickleness of the outside climate, researching
their ideas, responsible for the continuation of their livelihood?

She had asked the others briefly at work, knowing that
John Helton and his sister Sandi ran the place. Their parents
were now long gone, although details hadn't been particularly
forthcoming, as if she was not yet local enough to know such
information, but the farm was wealthy enough, with a healthy
flock, a reputation for thoroughbred rams and the small
shorthorn herd. Certainly enough sheep to make life particularly
hectic during the lambing season, she pondered.

* * *

Gill did not see Sandi again until one evening, about a
fortnight later, at the small supermarket in the high street. She
had ducked in out of a heavy rain shower, after parking on the
return journey from a hilltop farm, aware that the refrigerator
back at the cottage was looking particularly empty. Shaking the
rain from a waterproof and already hunting for some inspiration
on the grocery shelves, she had failed to notice the tall figure in
a work-stained, waxed olive-green jacket in the sizeable queue.
It was not until she had heaved a heavy basket, loaded with
essentials, to the back of the queue and wearily stared at the line
of waiting customers, that she registered who might be ahead
of her.

Sandi had turned around at the characteristic sound of a
basket clanking with a wine bottle and catching Gill's eye had
thrown her a grin. However, suddenly aware of the intervening

people in the queue she had let the smile slide away and had turned to face forward again. Gill had managed a brief nod of acknowledgement. But that was it.

CHAPTER FOUR

A new life—the first decision on the path

"Hello. Redbridge Veterinary Practice, Gill speaking."

"Oh, yeah, thanks, this is Sandi Helton. I'm having a nightmare with one of our best ewes…"

Gill missed a second or two in time as she digested the information. *Sandi Helton, struggling with a lambing, late in the evening*! It had been Gill's turn to be on call, not unusual as the new girl earning her place in the practice. And a suitable moment to try to stay calm and impress, she thought.

Within an hour of the call, they were in the warmth of one of the sheep barns facilitating perfectly delivered triplets, one definitely smaller than the others, but absolutely and beautifully alive. Gill found herself delighted not only with the generous heating of this particular outbuilding, but also the opportune moment to be called out to perform at this particular farm.

Sandi rubbed the lambs down with an old towel, clucking at them affectionately, the ewe butting her hands away nervously while making a low rumbling noise in her throat.

"They're all right pet. They're just fine…"

She looked pointedly across at Gill, who was drying off her arms. Despite trying to keep her eyes solely on the lambs she was managing to glow with barely suppressed pride. There was no denying that a little friction, like a low frequency background hum, had hung in the air between them throughout the proceedings.

"…thank you." Sandi finished.

"Well, you did all right yourself. Called me in quickly and delivered the first one."

"Ay well, she was no trouble. It was just her brothers that were causing it. Typical brothers…" she said with a wry smile. "You'll come inside for a drink, won't you? You deserve it after all that and such a god-awful time to be called out. I'm sorry for that…" This was the longest speech she had given in front of Gill since their first awkward meeting at The Hounds some months before, despite almost bumping into and then pointedly avoiding speaking to her in the queue at the Spar mini-market in Blackford, where the vicar and half of the village seemed to be waiting for service. But now, in truth, the barriers were down. Gill could see that she thought a great deal of this ewe, relaying to her how she had reared her by hand, relating the way she and John had helped her after a dog-worrying incident.

She seemed chuffed to bits to have seen Gill work. Gill had given the delivery her full attention. Calm, efficient and absorbed with the animals. Trying everything to keep her concentration from wandering.

"Thanks. That would be nice. And as for the time…I was up anyway and on duty. Reading…swotting actually. Some new drug catalogue that Bridget wanted to run past me. It was a welcome relief…" Gill looked at her watch. She could spare a half hour, couldn't she?

"Grand." Sandi held out her hand to pull Gill to her feet. "Thanks. Good job." She pulled Gill into an unexpected bear hug, her normal reserve suddenly overpowered by the occasion, or so it seemed to Gill. "That animal means the world. Come on to the house."

Gill turned, reeling a little from the sudden entanglement and the unexpected spark of pleasure inside her at the prospect of prolonging her visit. She packed up her equipment, trying not to look thrilled from the comforting physical contact, feeling very satisfied with her work, heaving the bag over her shoulder. Sandi led the way, after shutting the gates and fastening the barn door behind them, crossing the frosty old cobbles in an easy lope to the welcome glow and warmth of the farmhouse. She pushed open the door, holding it back to let Gill pass through, as if conscious of her closeness as she brushed by, both of them unable to look at each other this time, reminiscent as it was of that first meeting. If Gill was conscious of it too, she had not fully admitted it. They stopped to pull off their boots before stepping into the room.

"That's better." Sandi wriggled her toes. "Pop your bag down. What can I get you? Beer? Cuppa?"

"I need the bathroom first. Tea please, though."

"Just down the hall on the left."

The inside of the house was pleasing—warm, homely and tidy. Gill wondered to herself how they managed, if they were both out working on the farm.

The fire was still glowing when she returned to the living room where she found Sandi adding a log to beef it up and fend off the chill of the early spring night.

"John's out for the night. Meeting Lisa, I reckon, though he claims it's just so he can get into the market early tomorrow to check out the rams. He can't pull the wool over my eyes that easily." She chuckled, liking her own joke, apparently glad, too, to clear the air by getting her brother's absence off her chest early on.

Gill flopped into the cushions on an old settle by the fire, casting her eyes around the kitchen that showed few signs of changing in the last hundred years, apart from some power points, useful gadgets such as the discreetly placed coffeemaker, dishwasher and washing machine in the far corner, but still displaying relics such as the old-fashioned hooks hanging from the low beams. She noticed Sandi had to duck in places as she made her way around.

"Oh, Lisa? Of course. Have they been seeing each other for long?"

"Only since the school playground, pigtails and all!"

"That's sweet."

"Yeah, on and off, but mostly on for years. I think he kept the lid on it in front of Mum and Dad, as if they didn't know really."

"Why would he need to hide it?"

"Pa was afraid he'd uproot himself. He needed him. Pa could be a bit…assertive sometimes."

Gill let the implication lie. "But it wouldn't *have* to mean uprooting himself?"

"No, it wouldn't have. But it meant we both had something in common though. Something to hide from the parents." She paused to consider the statement and then changed the subject abruptly. "So you said tea? Or wine? There's some dandelion or a bottle I haven't opened from the summer raffle…"

"Cuppa, please. I've got to drive back down…and who knows…be called out again before breakfast. It is lambing season, as if I needed to tell you that!"

"Yeah, I haven't exactly had a full week's sleep."

"I bet. That makes two of us."

"And most of the stockholders in the county!" Sandi guffawed awkwardly.

There was a moment of uncomfortable silence that seemed to last a lifetime.

Gill dug around for further conversation. "How's it been going for you generally?"

"Trouble free mostly. A few we've had to watch over, that is until tonight." She recovered herself and pottered around the kitchen in a relaxed fashion, pulling out mugs and a teapot, laying out a tray with a feminine precision that surprised Gill, seeming to contrast with the physical confidence, the muscular easiness that she had witnessed so far, around the farm, the market, the village. She caught herself dwelling on the pictures filed away in her memory as she watched her and then suddenly became conscious again, *realizing* she had filed them, gone over them, let this woman play on her mind. She had been glad to hear the voice on the end of the phone a few hours earlier, delighted even to be able to come here, to the farm, confident in her ability to be useful and prove herself.

"Biscuits?" Sandi broke across her thoughts.

"Please!" Her socked feet were thawing out nicely, like her barrier between mixing work and pleasure. She pushed them out towards the fire, stretching her legs.

She noticed Sandi watching her, flashing her eyes up briefly whilst feigning concentration on the teapot. She carried the tray over and laid it out, filling the mugs, settling herself into the sofa opposite.

"Help yourself. Everyone likes it a bit different."

"Too right. Weak and feeble Southerner me!"

"Ah, I doubt that really."

Their stares coincided, until appearing embarrassed, Sandi broke the moment and looked away into the fire.

"I'm sorry I couldn't speak to you the other week."

"Oh, it's fine."

"I just didn't know what to say...in front of the vicar of all people."

"Why?"

"He was in the queue you realize. He's so shrewd. I thought I'd give myself away...if I spoke to you. He'd know."

"Know?"

Sandi ignored the prompt. "I don't know if he does. Ma always said I should be careful around people. Not everyone would understand. The church in particular. But hell to that really. I've kept myself to myself. I don't want to rub people up. But I am who I am and I'm not making a point of hiding it for anyone. People guess, I s'pose. I just get so fed up with people trying to pigeonhole everyone."

"And you'd give yourself away if you spoke to *me*?"

Sandi flushed to the roots of her hair.

Gill's heart went out to her again. This giant of a Yorkshire woman, fit, capable, overflowing with warmth...perhaps lonely too? *Perhaps it isn't easy to have a social life whether a vet or a farmer?*

"I don't particularly like labels either, trying to fit people into a box of 'normality', but if he's that shrewd he'd have noticed the electricity in the air…"

The dark brown eyes raised themselves to hers again in surprise and a sheepish grin spread endearingly.

Gill sipped her tea mock-daintily and then grinned back. "You think I haven't noticed you? Leaning at the bar, loading sheep effortlessly, leaping gazelle-like over the stiles and dry-stone walls? Veterinary College isn't a convent you know! We are allowed to have time to develop."

Confusion passed briefly through those features that showed themselves as naturally as the curve of the hillsides, the fall of the water in the tumbling springs. "And I thought you'd have had your head in your books all the time. You had time for a lot of 'development' there?"

"Only to learn…grow…you know…*find*. There was a fit Norwegian girl, but, well, she had to go back home, and I wasn't too sorry. Inga. A bit uptight for my liking. We're still sort-of friends. We still chat online occasionally. But we talk more about work now, difficult cases and clients, rather than anything else."

Sandi didn't reply.

"And you? When did *you* have time for anything? How could you find out here?"

Sandi looked offended, fleetingly. "What's wrong with here?"

"Nothing's wrong with here. Here is fantastic, beautiful, awesome in the true sense of the word. A place where you *have* to respect nature. But what chance do you have to break from convention?"

Sandi found her grin again. "Oh, I don't know…a fumble here, a nightclub over there maybe." She nodded vaguely in the direction of York. "Nothing much, enough to know, but nothing to worry about."

"And you said John had to keep his head down!"

"Well, you can't breathe in the village without everyone knowing. I *have* been allowed to escape the valley sometimes…" she added wryly.

"No I don't suppose you can do anything much in the village without it becoming common knowledge."

"Not with Rita about!"

They chuckled. They both knew Rita, one of the counter staff at the bakery, famed for being the fountain of all village news.

"But as for not being able to breathe in the village...I'm finding it kind of hard to breathe at all." Gill added, holding the startled gaze of the woman across the room. Her heart thudded in her throat.

The statement had come out suddenly, uncontrolled, the thought presenting itself unselfconsciously from her mind to her lips initially, her thoughts catching up afterwards. She checked herself momentarily, breaking away from the gaze and looking into her cup. This hadn't quite been the plan for her time at Blackford. Was she taking advantage of the generous hospitality on offer? She felt a moment of confusion as her heart hammered in her throat. Surely it must be audibly giving her away? She glanced up again, catching a smile passing across her companion's mouth. With sudden clarity, she realized that it wasn't her move to make—a visitor, a professional in this place tonight. Her indecision continued to waver.

It was Sandi who uncurled herself and crossed the room to sit down next to Gill, brushing a piece of hair from her face and tucking it behind her ear tidily.

"Now I'm afraid I might be transgressing the work/client boundaries," Gill continued, almost in a whisper.

Sandi sighed, an apparently unconscious sigh escaping her as Gill watched her transferring the mug from one hand to the other, setting it down on the floor, to take Gill's hand in hers, almost in slow motion, her palm flat, not yet fully committed. Gill threaded her fingers lightly into the offered hand, spreading the fingers slightly apart in doing so. This gentle gesture motivated a further response from Sandi, who turned to look at her, and releasing Gill's hand, slid her arm along the top of the sofa, behind her, bringing her head close enough to lean forwards to touch her lips on the cheekbone on one side.

Pausing to consider addressing the other side, and then Gill was turning towards her, encouraging her with a soft, eager mouth meeting hers.

"Ah…" The gentle sigh from Sandi spoke subconsciously of a period of waiting. Gill heard it. She pulled away to look searchingly into the face that had enchanted her from that first moment. The warm brown eyes flooded her with empathy.

"I knew it. I knew it when you walked into the bar with Jim and the others, that first evening. I'd been here six weeks and thought I'd signed myself up to the back of beyond and then you walked in. I mean I didn't know, but I hoped…"

She grinned. "You hoped right…"

"And then in the corridor later…something instinctively told me…"

Sandi nodded, "I thought so…" The strong hands were feeling their way across her shoulders and back. "My God, you're lovely. This isn't *actually* breaking some professional ethical code is it?"

Gill laid her head against Sandi's shoulder and smiled, breathing in the smell of new hay, fresh air and what was that hovering in the background…honesty? She nuzzled into the neck, still tanned from a season ago of working in the sunshine. "We're both adults aren't we?"

Sandi turned to her and kissed her fully, pushing her back onto the sofa next to her, seemingly only too glad to find her enthusiasm returned, hands fighting their way beneath shirts, following the shapes of hips, waists and breasts.

"You're on call?"

"Yes, but you don't get a reduced deal for this." She grinned, teasing her. "Seriously though, my mobile's on the answerphone. And…it's turning into a fiendishly difficult delivery at Helton Farm."

Sandi grinned, hauled herself upright and offered her hand. "Well, bring the phone and come this way…if you like, that is. You haven't seen the rest of the house…" Vaguely she offered up a smoke-screen alternative.

Sandi walked over to the front door and drew the bolt across. Gill grinned at her, as she picked herself up off the sofa, not bothering to rearrange herself. She rummaged for her phone in her bag, checking the signal was good and took it in one hand, the other hand finding Sandi's to be led out of the kitchen into the rear of the house and up the generous staircase towards the privacy of a bedroom.

Once there Sandi drew the curtains across the darkness beyond the window and switched on a lamp, revealing a surprisingly tidy, pastel-colored room with an enormous bed covered by a homely patchwork quilt.

"My room," she said simply, almost coyly, although less coyly turned to the task of unbuttoning Gill's shirt.

"My legs have gone weak."

"Come here then." Sandi swooped her up as easily as she would have picked up a troublesome animal and took her to the bed, laying her there. She pulled herself onto the bed next to her, propping herself up on an elbow, looking serious, and traced the outline of her face with the back of her free hand. Finding only a look of encouragement, Sandi continued along the line of Gill's neck, down to the lowest available patch of skin at the bottom of the open neckline of her shirt. Gill watched, caressing Sandi's arm and side lightly. She felt herself thinking how easy it all was, with no great fuss, as if it was the most natural thing in the world to be led to a bedroom and to go from drinking tea to pulling each other's clothes off. Sandi loosened the shirt, following the skin a little lower. She smiled. Gill's shirt was now spread open, revealing a hastily thrown on vest.

"I dressed for the cold…"

"As if I care…" Sandi had started to feel her way up her jeans to the buttons at the top, loosening them. Gill briefly battled with some self-consciousness, remembering how she had dressed hurriedly, earlier in the day. Her jeans slipped easily down her legs as Sandi pulled at them, pants coming too in the tug-of-war, leaving Gill free, bare, alarmingly exposed, not quite ready for the warm, hungry hands that now explored her gently and felt her, first under the vest, then to warm, wet, open desire that welcomed curious fingers with their inquisitive stroking until the fire spread unbearably across her.

"And I thought it was me who led the way…" Gill gasped.

"Mm?" Sandi responded, busy, preoccupied. "You think?" She grinned up at her from her position, now knelt beside her, then ducked her head slowly, bringing her tongue into play.

"Oh my…unfair…"

Sandi stopped. "Unfair?"

"Only because I need to touch you, too."

Sandi smirked and pulled herself upright again beside her, stretching, wriggling out of her already disheveled clothes with Gill's help, until they lay facing each other, naked in the warm room, faces on a level with each other. Gill took in Sandi's muscular body, shaped by continuous work, taut, but not muscle-bound. Gill reached a hand into the small of Sandi's back, pulling their torsos closer together, literally seeking bodily warmth, touching at the breast, hips, thighs. Gill was overwhelmed with a powerful throbbing sensation from her lower abdomen. Lying opposite, their mouths found each other easily. There was a lull as they each contemplated the prospect and perhaps, only fleetingly, its personal significance. How beautifully fitting the meeting of those warm lips, the tongues brushing across them and touching. A fierce burning had woken inside Gill. Warm breasts pressing warm breasts, nipples erect towards each other and brushing each other with waves of sensuous pleasure. Their hands reached down to find each other's inviting warmth, both gasping breaths inwards at the first welcome, surprising touch of experimental fingers, parting, exploring, delving.

"Oh help," Gill whispered.

"What?" Sandi murmured.

"I'm afraid of…"

"Me? Ha!"

"No…"

"Stop thinking for a moment will you?"

"Gladly…I'm afraid of how it all ends…"

"It doesn't have to," Sandi murmured back. And hands now pulsated rhythmically, pushing wave upon wave, breaking over and around them, until the world's intrusions were all gone, receding into nothing compared to this moment, this here and now, this present purity, need and desire. Sandi's other arm reached around Gill. A warm hand on her back pulling her close in. Gill felt she might explode with pleasure as she kissed her neck, her warm skin, following a path that went over the breasts, dwelling on their peaks, curling around them, following, wriggling her way down.

"I *have* to taste you."

Sandi groaned as Gill's tongue and lips found their way across her to where she arched tensely.

"Oh my…"

Gill pushed her legs gently wider and Sandi spread herself to draw her in, bending around to reach with a free hand to where she could delve into Gill's warmth.

"Bendy too…" Gill chuckled.

"It's all the exercise. Oh…" She shuddered, further conversation impossible.

Only when they were exhausted, did they fall back onto the cool sheets, bodies hot, bedclothes pushed to the edges of the bed. And Gill's phone had not rung yet.

"Am I…safe to stay for a moment more?" Gill managed through settling breaths.

"Stay…as long as you want…please." Sandi responded softly, the request sounding endearing. "I've never had anyone to stay." She pulled the bedspread over them.

"Then I will…but I may have to go if the phone—"

"I know…"

Further words and touches were more excruciating than bearable then, and they fell asleep still tangled together.

Gill woke in the night. Disorientated, although Sandi's presence feeling safe near her. The phone had not gone again, but she was on call and it might ring. She was suddenly wide awake, afraid of waking Sandi with a start, of breaking their capsule of delightfulness with a sudden call to reality. What if John had changed his plans and returned unexpectedly? What if the signal was weak and she was missing something urgent? Her car alone was enough to give her away around here and what awkwardness would it cause for Sandi?

What curtain-twitchers in the village might notice her car not returning again all night?

She crept out of the bed, careful not to move the sheet or creak the mattress. She did not want to distress Sandi when she woke to find her gone, so she crept downstairs to the kitchen and hunted in her bag for paper and a pen.

Thanks. Have to go. Hope this is just a beginning...G x

She left the paper on the pillow where she had been lying. Sandi lay peacefully on the other side of the bed. A chink of moonlight lit her from a gap in the curtains. A tremor passed through Gill as she watched, longing to kiss her again. Only time would tell. She felt joy coursing through her veins, and thankfully no hint of guilt or embarrassment. So sudden...so perfect.

CHAPTER FIVE

The start of the climb

Working at Meadow Farm the next morning, Gill was cornered for a conversation by the owner's son. He had been lounging on the bar gate while she dealt with an infection in a sow's ear. Having introduced himself as Andrew, he proceeded to give off the confident and relaxed aura of someone who had never needed to worry about money, or even perhaps anybody disliking him. He was evidently handsome and sure of himself, still finishing off his final year of university, wondering what to do afterwards he said, perhaps only too glad to stay and take on some responsibilities at the farm. The easy route he said, though Gill had doubted that. The life of the Dales farmers was hardly an easy one she pointed out to him. Andrew was more of her generation than many of the other villagers. It was effortless to fall into conversation with him, until out of the blue he took a more personal approach.

"Would you like a trip to Angle Tarn on one of your days off? I could show you some of the local sights?"

"Erm, well, that would be very nice." She felt she had better make herself clear from the start. "But you do know I'm only looking for friends don't you?" Her petite and feminine looks had misled the opposite sex many times before.

"Er, yeah, of course." He sounded doubtful, even slightly confused.

"It's just that…well…don't make too much of this to anyone…but I'm batting for the other side, if you know what I mean." *God, how much easier it would be if there was a label or a sign you could give to make yourself clear.*

"Oh." He paused to think for a moment. "Cool. Lucky them."

She laughed at him.

"Thank heavens. Broad-mindedness in the narrow valley!"

He grinned back at her. "We're not all small-town small-minded."

"Hooray. I'm a bit cautious. I don't want to rub anyone up the wrong way." She finished with the wound on the ear and climbed over the pen to pack away.

He grinned. "You'll probably find there's less of a problem with that than you think. People give off an air of normality, but you come across just as much variety in the villages as the towns. Live here long enough and the private lives start to spill out."

She was beginning to like him more.

"Anyway, the offer still stands. We could take a drive in the convertible jeep over the hills on a fair weather day and I'll point out some good places to hang out in town. There's a shortage of quality younger company around here. I get it, you know. Had an eclectic mix of friends at uni. But if you find any cute gals who want to play for my team, let me know!"

She gave him an amicable grin. It sounded like a good offer. She liked it that he was quick thinking.

"Thanks. We'll do that when I get a chance. New 'gal' at the practice. I'm on call one in three weekends."

"Do you need to wash up at the house? Come and see if the parents are about?"

"Just the outdoor tap will do thanks, I need to press on. I've a list of calls that will take me into the afternoon."

"Another time. Give me a call when you want to head out of the valley, when it starts to freak you out!"

As she drove away from the farm and the car climbed up the opposite side of the fell away from Blackford, affording a glimpse of Helton Farm, Gill needed to pinch herself in disbelief. Did that *really* just happen last night? The fog of tiredness hung over her, as if she had been at an all-night party, sleepless into the early hours. But *that* was a familiar feeling. That was her afterworld of many a weekend on call, where nightshifts could mean running out to an emergency difficult foaling, calving, lambing or other similar problem. The ache around her heart and somewhere in the base of her abdomen, the unexpected throb at the acknowledgment of the memory of the night's adventure, these were less familiar feelings, not uncomfortable, just surprising. A door opened in her time in the Dales that she had planned to keep closed. She stopped the car at a lay-by on the hilltop, stepped slightly wearily out of the vehicle and stood, letting the sharp, cold air blast her. The shocking chill flooded through her, reviving her enough for the tasks ahead. She looked back the way the car had climbed, and felt gratitude, with only the tiniest hint of fear that she may have complicated her world. Only a little fear though, outweighed by, and perhaps morphing into, excitement and anticipation. She shuddered, losing track of whether it was the cold or her feelings that caused the shiver. Back to work, the other would have to wait, but for now she could delve into a private compartment of memories to enhance her day.

CHAPTER SIX

The call back

The phone rang about six times and Gill's heart was starting to sink when it was picked up suddenly, and an efficient but jovial male voice chimed in, "Helton Farm, hello?"

"Oh, hi. Is that John? It's Gill from Redbridge. Is Sandi in, I wanted to check how the triplets are doing?"

She hoped the question sounded plausible.

"Hello!" John's voice relaxed. "Ah, Gill. Thanks very much for the job you did there. They're doin' great. No problems, settling in nicely. Our ewe recovered fast too. Took them all on board without a backward glance." Gill was starting to worry he would fill her in completely when he added, "Hang on…"

She heard him pull away from the receiver to call his sister. "Sandi! It's the vet's, checking on Tammy and her lambs…"

Gill heard a clatter and footsteps on the kitchen tiles.

"Hi!" Sandi's voice, warm and deep.

"Hi! How are the lambs and…Tammy? That's sweet…a sweet name."

"They're absolutely fine. Settling in…no problems."

"John…is he out of earshot."

"He's just gone out to the barn."

"You okay? I'm sorry I left in the middle of the night. I had a sudden feeling he might come back and then there would be some explaining to do."

"I'm fine. But I missed you in the empty space that you left. And your note…'Thanks'…like I'd given you a present? Or helped you across the road?"

"Well, you did…both actually."

There was a silence as they digested their statements.

"I would have called sooner, but I've been half dead on my feet and rushed off them too at work."

"And I did call the surgery. But they said you were out on rounds," Sandi added.

"You did? They didn't say. Come to think about it I didn't go back in when I finished, I just headed home and keeled over for an hour."

The sound of Sandi chuckling quietly came down the line.

"See? See what you did to me?" Gill smiled.

"And you think I've been any better? Well, at least I've had a skip in my step all day as I checked on the lambing. That little family of triplets will hold a special place, I can tell you…"

"So…will you come out for a meal with me? Not tonight, as I'm deadbeat. But soon? Tomorrow? I'm free this weekend. We can go to town."

"John owes me one after me holding the fort last night and—he thinks—having a tough time with the triplets."

"That's what you said?"

"I had to explain my tiredness."

"As it turns out you'll get two evenings for the price of one so to speak."

"That's what you're offering is it?"

"Let's see how the mood takes us."

Gill tingled at the thought. "Call me," she added, giving her mobile number, "when you have a free evening then."

"That'll be tomorrow evening then. Take my number, too." She relayed it.

"Tomorrow then? I'll pick you up."

"Come to the end of the lane at six. Let's keep John in the dark, at least for a while."

A while. That was promising. It indicated a duration of time, a continuation and a fulfillment.

CHAPTER SEVEN

First date—skirting round the edges

Gill pulled her car into the lay-by at the bottom of the lane and switched off the lights. The village lay sparkling in the approaching dusk like a late Christmas decoration at the bottom of the valley. Her heart thudded with nervous anticipation, hoping that everything would fall into place, wondering whether she had overdressed for the evening. She had asked Becka quietly about the best restaurants just out of the local area and had been advised on a choice of two in Allerdale. She had booked a table in both, hoping Sandi would help her to choose.

Soon a tall, loping figure appeared at the corner of the lane, descending steadily down to the car.

Sandi opened the passenger door and ducked down to get in, surprising Gill with a denim skirt cut above the knee and some rather delicious legs. She tossed a leather jacket into the footwell.

"Hi!" Gill barely managed to say before her mouth was enclosed in a soft, hungry kiss that sent encouraging shivers all over her again.

"How about we skip the meal?" Sandi said huskily.

"No." Gill was quietly firm. She caressed Sandi's cheek. "I want to get to know you."

"You know me pretty well after the other night!"

"You know exactly what I mean!" Gill smiled at her.

"Oh, okay." Sandi sighed comically, in a resigned but happy manner. "I suppose I am actually hungry for something to eat, too."

"But that means you're free...allowed out for the night?" Gill felt a surge of elated anticipation.

"We're not joined at the hip y'know. He's not me Dad!" Sandi chuckled at her.

"Right." She started the car, maneuvered back down the lane and joined the road to head away from Blackford.

"So...John...he knows. About you I mean."

"Yeah. I had to explain myself to him. After we lost Mum and Dad. I didn't want him thinking he'd lose me too. I told him he was probably stuck with me as a partner in the farm and a stockwoman because there was no way I was upping and marrying some daft bugger from the village and having their kids and washing, cleaning and cooking for them, because that just wasn't and never had been my scene. To which he asked precisely what my scene was, as y'know it was taking a second for the penny to drop fully, and I made it clear to him what had been going on with me while he was busy being preoccupied in Lisa Blackwell's knickers. To which he finally laughed at me and said wouldn't I like to know what went on there."

Gill was chuckling and trying not to swerve off the road as she cast sideways glances.

"Mind how yer drive. It was these roads that finished them off. Mum and Dad, I mean."

"Oh shit. I'm so sorry. I hadn't heard exactly what happened."

"Don't bother yourself too much. It's been six years now. Enough time to get used to the idea. Though it wasn't that easy at the time. And you never completely get over that stuff I'm told. We were pretty young and many people thought we wouldn't be able to make a go of the farm. We had some good offers. But John and I, we weren't going to jack it in that easily. It was everything they had built up. We'd seen how hard they worked. The risks they took."

Silence fell for a while.

She added softly, "And it was a bloody tourist. Pulling out without looking. It made them swerve. P'r'aps they were goin' too fast. That's what the inquest said. Put them right into a head-on collision, avoiding the path of a delivery lorry. The tourists didn't make it either. They careered down the hill. I have to drive past the spot every so often."

"Hell. I'm so sorry."

"Yeah, well, life's like that sometimes. A bit of a bitch."

Silence fell. Gill struggled to find the right thing to say. Fortunately Sandi continued.

"Working on a farm all your life, you see the unfairness of it sometimes."

"I can go with you on that one. I've seen animals that didn't deserve the treatment or the end that came to them."

"Exactly. But you pick yourself up and carry on because the daffodils and the lambs still come in spring and the sun's warm on your back again and the fire crackles in the hearth and the beer's good at The Hounds and the unexpected laughter in a day makes the world right again, and then one day a bloody gorgeous vet from York arrives."

Gill leant her arm across and squeezed the firm thigh next to her. Sandi reached across to ruffle her hair in response.

"Careful…I spent hours arranging that."

"As if you need to! Mmm." Sandi lightened her mood. "So this isn't the road I was expectin'. Where are we off to?"

"Okay. We have a choice. I was cheeky and booked into two different places. I have been strongly advised"—she cleared her throat in mock-importance—"by Becka, no less, of course not telling her quite what I was up to, that the places to be for a hot date slash romantic evening meal of a Friday night round here without mixing it up with the rowdy crowd, are…wait for it… either Bel Ami, gourmet hotspot or The Horse and Cart. I serve that ball to you and await your return."

Sandi smirked at the delivery. "Well, let me see. I know at least two of the bar staff in The Horse and Cart…"

"Oh!" Gill sounded disappointed.

"You forget what a small pond you've arrived in…but I don't know anything about the other, have never eaten there and think that's our best bet. At least for some privacy."

"Great. Will you take my phone and call the pub to cancel then? The number's on recent calls."

"Sure. Will do."

Gill noticed Sandi had no trouble with her latest model phone.

"You're not a technophobe?"

"Huh?"

"Sorry, Southerners' talk for gadgets."

"Cheeky! John's a fan of technology. We're pretty up to speed at Helton Farm, don't you know?" Sandi mocked her accent carefully, cautious of going too far. She was underestimating Gill's ability to be teased: it was one of her pleasures in life to be with someone she trusted enough for them to laugh at each other as well as with each other. Gill noticed the way her Yorkshire accent came and went with her mood or each different turn of phrase.

"Did you ever go away to study?"

"Yep. I was in my third year at Aberystwyth when the accident happened. Agricultural Studies and Management, of course."

"Crumbs. So you stopped?"

"Missed half a term. Came back to finish and pulled off an upper second. Lord knows how under the circumstances. I think it helped me to blank things out. Just concentrating. And I knew John needed me. But needed me to be good at what I did for the sake of the farm. He managed while I was away for that term with the help of the fellas in the valley. They're a bloody good lot when you need them. Frank still comes up an' works most of the week."

"That's quite inspiring. I don't know much about you really, do I?"

"Oh, I think you're starting to find out. And what about you? Here I am rabbiting on, you're getting me to talk and I want to know about you."

"Well, what do you want to know?"

"Anything that's on offer."

"So...two parents."

"That's not abnormal."

"Living just outside Hereford."

"That's more normal than me."

"A few livestock, nothing on your scale though. Mum's a teacher actually, Geography, Dad plays at being a smallholder but really is retired from the police, did thirty years' service and now runs a small business selling gardening equipment, seeds and plants from the garden shed."

"A copper's daughter?"

"Yeah, that's a story. I was brought up terrified of putting a foot wrong. Found I loved animals, worked at the local animal rescue center as a volunteer when I was old enough. The folks put me through college, seven excruciating years for them, but they came into a little inheritance, which made it bearable. I came out to them in my second year at college. Dad nearly choked on the spot. Mum worked her magic and brought him around, that is, after he struggled to speak to me for a term. I think it was just embarrassment and dissolving dreams. Then he became pretty right on about it all and even has been known to defend me. After college I worked a year out in a South African reserve, paid luckily, then landed my first permanent position in York through a friend of a friend."

"I heard about Africa. That's been around the village already. *'She can't half work some magic on me bulls and cows, what were she like with those bull elephants?'* Your stories have been batted around."

"Heck and a half."

"Quite."

"What else? I thought I was nearly going to be cornered by Andrew down at Meadow Farm yesterday. He was watching me while I sorted out their sow and the chat turned friendly. I had to give him a few clues..."

"He's decent though. I bet he took it on board. For all his foppish charms, he can be a bit of a rock."

"Yeah. So he came across. Still wanted to show me the sights of Angle Tarn regardless."

"Did he now?"

They laughed. The black, forbidding moorland swept away on both sides of the road with only an occasional passing car or outlying, remote farm lighting the night. It was easy to see how an accident might happen. The full beam headlights lit up the tarmac and drystone walls as the road started to descend into another valley. The friendly lights of Allerdale beckoned from the valley floor.

"Mind out for the hairpin bend in a minute. You'll like Allerdale. You haven't been yet?"

Gill shook her head. "Nope."

"Market on Tuesday, lovely old-fashioned stone square, the streets cluster around it and sort of expand outwards, like ever-increasing circles. The restaurant will be on the high street. I've seen it but never been in."

"Until tonight. Parking?"

"On the sides of the market square. Should be fine. It's not like we're back in York."

"Yes York, now come to think of it you mentioned nightclubs in York. We might have been breathing the same air of a Saturday night?"

"Possibly. But this was more before your time there I reckon. I went a bit nuts, had to let some steam off when I was back in the valley for good."

"Do I need to be jealous?"

"Nothing serious or too much for you to wonder about. Do I?"

"Nope. I'm just a bit envious *I* didn't meet you then. I'm trying to imagine whether you're a good mover."

"Don't you know that yet?"

"Dancing, you big nelly."

"I need *some* surprises up me sleeve."

"Aberystwyth? Was that fun?"

"A mixture. I can be a bit of a loner sometimes. Got the chance to swim with dolphins though."

"*Dolphins?*"

"It was a fluke really. Driving past on a coast road, I could see some not far out. It was remote really. Pulled up, stripped off, went in. Bloody cold. But they were curious, they came up and nosed me a bit. It was a calm day and the sun was getting warmer. We played for a bit and then went our separate ways."

"Wow…you do realize how rare that is, don't you? Wild dolphins!"

"Yeah, I guess it was one of those lucky chances. A privilege."

They were among the streetlights of the town now and Sandi navigated them to the square where they parked up and alighted. Gill tossed her bag onto her shoulder; Sandi slung her jacket on and then reached for Gill's hand. They grinned at each other. Gill wondered briefly, though uncaringly, whether they made an unusual-looking couple to the locals. No one batted an eyelid though. There were dog-walkers, groups of pub-goers and other Friday night couples drifting around the streets. Sandi grinned at her and led them along to the bistro.

She opened the door and Gill stepped in first. She noticed Sandi's glancing sweep of the room and wondered whether it caused her any concern that she might know someone. Apparently all was satisfactory and Sandi appeared quite relaxed. Perhaps she was casting about for their privacy rather than anything else.

A quiet table in a booth screened by plants played host to them for the evening. Light meals of the house special quiche and salad, a glass of wine each and shared desserts, laughter and increasingly familiar conversation passed an hour or two, serving to make them both aware that this was surely only an aching aperitif.

They had agreed that coffee at Gill's would round the evening off nicely, conscious of the euphemism and giggling together, they wrapped the meal up quickly, settling the bill and heading for home, light in mood, heavy in anticipation. Sandi had said that she was curious, too, to see inside Gill's little house and to be able to picture her there.

They pulled the car up by the cottage at the mill, letting themselves in quietly through the backdoor. Gill drew curtains and flicked on lamps, revealing her sparse belongings, some still packed boxes of books, a few items of tasteful furniture and souvenirs that she had accumulated on her travels. But the coffee was never made. The introductory tour went immediately from hurried mouthed kissing and wrestling with clothing in the living room directly to the upper floor viewing via the bathroom to the double-bedded gallery.

Gill had worn a light dress for the night, bare feet beneath her zipped boots, now removed and little else, other than the dress and a light jacket, apart from silk panties underneath. She had taken a moment or two to consider these in front of the mirror before she left and had gone for the unabashed purple ones. Now, Sandi unzipped the dress and let it slide, the two women standing facing each other at the foot of the bed, curtains tightly drawn, a single lamp lit near the window.

"Oh, my." Sandi stood and simply stared for a moment. "A vision of loveliness."

Gill's heart was thumping in her chest as she took the single step towards her. She ran her hand down from Sandi's tidy waist to the hem of the skirt and slid underneath.

"You make me so wet, I can hardly bear the wait," Sandi murmured.

"That's my line of thought." Gill sighed softly into her ear, feeling her way round with her lips to the sweet mouth that eagerly awaited her at the same time that she felt her way up the inside of Sandi's thigh to the lack of underwear that greeted her.

"You temptress."

"These, however, are staying on for me to play with for a moment." Sandi referred to the purple pants and slid down Gill a little way to run her fingers over them and brush her lips against them.

"Mmm. Silk?"

"Only the best for you, darling," Gill mimicked.

Sandi chuckled hoarsely and slid her tongue and then her fingers inside the fabric, making Gill groan until she had to pull on her hard to lever her back up to eye level and put Sandi back within reach of her own hands.

"Oh you beautiful woman," she sighed, feeling her from her face, down her neck, following the line of collarbone, breast, to the peak of nipples, the curve of bosom, the fold of skin, the tautness of an abdomen that knew hard work every day, the unabashed forest of hair that housed the places of pleasure where her fingers knew instinctively where they wanted to go. Her lips locked onto Gill, as if hunting for a place to anchor in case reality was lost forever. Gill understood and received her so sensitively, opening herself with a frightening honesty to receive the fragile gift of a partner bared to the soul. She lightened her touch as Sandi cried out and trembled in temporary rigidity and loss of all control.

They lay quietly for a moment while the storm subsided for Sandi. Gill stroked the curve of her back gently. The deep trust fired her from inside creating a furnace that sought to kiss her again, with ever-deeper kisses until she felt the reviving touch of Sandi on her, returning the earnest compliment. And she opened herself, desiring her, drawing her in, glad to feel Sandi's legs locked around one of her thighs as her strong hand pushed the other away, spreading her and feeling over her with inquisitive hands and then surprising her with the sweetest touch of lips and investigative tongue, again and again, until she felt herself sliding into an inevitability that was so welcome and so relieving as to be daunting.

Strong, gentle hands comforted her along her sides as she gasped for breath and felt tears spilling from her eyes. Sandi hauled herself up to her mouth again and their mouths brushed each other repeatedly, stroking each other's bodies into submission, like surprised animals needing reassurance, eventually after quiet words to each other falling into a temporary sleep of recovery and peacefulness.

They woke again in the night, went to the kitchen, parched for drinks, bringing mugs of tea back to bed to lie there peacefully in each other's company, finally falling again into a deep slumber, tangled, contented.

CHAPTER EIGHT

Breaking dawn

The dawn light filtered through the curtains. Sandi woke first. She grinned to herself as the night's memories crowded in. Gill was there beside her. She was in Gill's house. They had passed through the barrier of privacy and bliss and lived to remember it, hopefully to repeat it. She stroked Gill's arm, but receiving only a minor movement of acknowledgment slid out of the bed, gathered the mugs and went to the kitchen. She worked out how to operate the coffee machine and put it on to warm, then went to shower in the downstairs bathroom. She was sat at the small kitchen table, wrapped in towels and hugging a mug of coffee when Gill appeared.

"Cold?"

"Hot shower, but yes, the air's chilly."

Gill flicked the thermostat up and the heating clicked on.

"I slept so heavily. Can't imagine why." She grinned. "Glad you've found your way around and made yourself at home." She let her hand rest lightly on Sandi's shoulder. "I suppose you have to get back?"

"Not exactly. I told John I was off to York yesterday. He was surprised as I haven't been there in forever."

"So you have a little longer?"

"I have all weekend. I said it was time I had a weekend off."

"Show him who wears the trousers!"

"Hah!" She reached up to squeeze Gill's hand.

"Want some breakfast?"

"Please."

"Anything in particular."

"Do you have eggs? Scrambled eggs, if you have them."

"Good call." She started to set to work preparing them. "Will you make me a coffee too please?"

"Sure."

"Here's the thing. I was lying up in bed wondering…what all this means for you? I mean if you had to walk out of my front door, first thing in the morning. Would that be a bother?"

In the midst of busying herself with another coffee, Sandi looked up and gave her a gentle grin, "Y'think that would bother me? Blimey I could shout it from the rooftops after last night."

Gill grinned, apparently enormously satisfied.

"It's not like I've ever tried really to be shy about myself and hide away. Only not to ram it down other folk's throats."

"I noticed. When you walked into The Hounds the first night I laid eyes on you. One strong woman amongst a group of rugged men."

"I think most people know or suspect it even if they don't think too hard about such stuff. People prefer not to think sometimes. It's not like I'm the only one."

"No?"

"There's you."

"Ha, ha."

"Actually there are the Misses Du Pont and Wilson."

"There are?"

"School teachers, living down at the Brook End."

"I haven't met them."

"They live a quiet life. Knitting, cats, and schoolbooks. Mind you, who knows what gymnastics go on behind that cottage door!"

Gill smirked as she stirred the eggs.

"The fellas tease me in a good-natured way too. If they're having a joke about Lucy behind the bar perhaps or something else, I'm usually invited in on it. I think they see me as one of them. I've sort of proved myself along the way. They've seen me wrestle their beasts or pin a sheep down at shearing time."

"Oh, how you turn me on."

Sandi was pleased that Gill saw through her, that being at ease with herself and belonging so firmly within her home environment seemed to send Gill's feelings racing rather than fleeing.

"Eggs please, I'm starving." Sandi laughed. The toast popped up as if on cue and they collapsed in giggles, recovering just enough to serve up some breakfast and eat.

Sandi's towels started to unravel towards the end of this, which involved Gill helping them to unravel and another trip to the comfortable bed upstairs for unfinished business, the savoring of newly showered skin for the one and the enjoyment of lingering perfumes of the night before for the other. This was another thing that appeared to please Gill. The fact that Sandi was straightforward, natural and unfettered, apparently fearless—or so she said—was proving to be a recurring attraction.

"So what to do for the day?" Gill wondered out loud, as she lay there.

"Just stay here forever." Sandi lay sprawled across the bed, barely covered by a tangled sheet.

"That has potential." Gill suggested. "Except for the very real danger of friction burns on several parts of my body."

Sandi slapped a hand on the mattress and laughed. "Oh, okay then. Save a little of yourself for later…there's another night to enjoy."

Gill sighed with satisfaction. "Very well. Spare me a minute then, while I go and freshen up. Have a think about what we could do beyond these four walls."

"I have some excellent ideas about what we could do and where we could do it already…"

Gill smirked at her as she departed for the shower.

Sandi lay on the bed and smiled to herself. Utter bliss. She curled her body in on herself, pulling the sheets that smelt of Gill over her. She could get to like this. This smooth-skinned, pert angel who had appeared out of the blue. Who hopefully wouldn't disappear into the blue again. She had seen a few people come and go through the valley, while she had stayed, and would stay a lifetime perhaps, apart from three hard-working and sometimes lonely years out at college. And still she had been back every holiday helping on the farm, often until her body ached. It ached now. Just in a different way. She grinned anew. She throbbed between her legs, as if Gill's touch hadn't stopped. She touched herself. Everything was ready to explode into flame at the drop of a hat. Hopefully she would be able to walk. A laugh burst out of her.

There had been three major girlfriends in her life so far and a few frantic flings, those she put down to her emotional mess for a while. The three began with Sally at school, who had moved away and simply disappeared off the radar. She still suspected parental involvement in that one. Then Ali at college, a sports fanatic, who wore her out with her desire for a morning jog or a game of squash at any opportunity, although not enough bedroom athletics for her liking. And most recently, Mel, from Allerdale. Sympathetic and a bit obsessive. She hadn't wanted to let go. Sandi had needed to try various tactics to make it clear that she had moved on from her choking emotional grip. That's why she had needed to avoid the pub and had to be sure there was no one familiar at the restaurant. She was pretty sure that Gill hadn't clocked it. Everything was sure to be okay eventually. It hadn't helped either that Sandi hadn't had the strength of will not to go back for another shag last time Mel had pleaded loneliness with her, on a chilly autumnal night in the not-so-distant past. But crikey, Sandi knew she wasn't saint enough to deny both of them, when she too was struggling and despairing of ever having the strength of character to really let it all go. She had been fair. She'd made it clear what she meant by it. And this was all before Gill had arrived.

Still, once Mel got wind of what was happening now, surely she would realize that was the finale? Surely she would finally believe it was time to let things go?

The others? Well they'd just been moments of comfort, insanity or neediness. The briefest of club snogs or fumbles, only rarely progressing onto waking up with a relative stranger the next morning in York. She knew she hadn't always been in control of herself. In fact needed probably to work her way through the fog of grief and confusion that had been her life for a while. Still, brief wrestles through lonely nights had filled the gap.

But she'd made sense of it all eventually. Somewhere along the line had some sudden moments of clarity. Where alcohol, the shallow comfort of someone she didn't really know or care that deeply about or exhaustion had left her even lonelier, empty and unfulfilled. Compared to the progress and small successes of the farm that made her want to shout from the tops of the fells with triumph. She'd gone for advice with a doctor in York, far from the gossip of the valley, knowing that she wasn't quite herself, and he had agreed that she was probably dealing with her grief this way, advising some time out, a short course of helpful medication, some reassessment of her priorities and a few medical checks to make sure she had not left herself with any lingering side effects.

Time had passed. And then this. A connection. Already this felt exquisitely different.

She made her mind up exactly where she wanted to take Gill today. A private place that she hadn't let anyone in on. Barrow Tarn and the falls. Where the water had carved its way over hundreds of years there was a series of troughs in the hillside. She knew it so well. The paths didn't come close without trying hard and it was possible to hide from view behind the rock-face if anyone came near.

She rolled out of bed, pleased with the decision, shrugged quickly into her clothes and went to make another coffee for both of them.

It took about three-quarters of an hour's drive to reach the lonely lay-by that she loved on the top of the moors, where the view unrolled in all directions, leaving you with the feeling of being on top of the world, the queen of the castle. The air was crystal clear, inclined to whip you on windy days, but today it was calm and fresh, the sun trying to give warmth at last after the frigidity of winter.

She grabbed Gill's hand enthusiastically, leading her over the dry stone-wall stile and into an empty field. Gill was exclaiming over the view, filling Sandi with satisfaction. They scrambled down a steeper path that became strewn with boulders, until turning into a basin in the hillside where the rainwater gathered at the permanent Barrow Tarn. It was always picturesque. Privately enclosed, with a beach of small gravel and flat shale stones closest to their approach. Sandi released Gill's hand and bent down to skim stones. Hers bounced several times and Gill competed playfully with her until they were counting and laughing at each slight advance and each disastrous attempt.

"Comin' in?" Sandi called, peeling off her socks.

"You're joking? It will be icy." Gill retreated to the grassy bank and flopped in the sunshine letting her jacket fall open to absorb the warmth of the sun's rays.

Sandi laughed and waded in. "Yep! Freezin'!" She backed out after a few moments and dried herself approximately, reapplying footwear. "Come on! This isn't all of it."

"There's more?" Gill hauled herself up again and followed Sandi, who was already scampering like a billy goat down a barely visible sheep track. She turned off abruptly sideways, towards the noise of a light waterfall and was gone over the rocks.

"Hang on!"

"You all right, sweetie?"

"I'm fine. I just don't want to lose you."

"You won't lose me, ever. Having trouble following me?" Sandi called.

"I'd follow you to the ends of the earth…today," Gill gasped back.

"Only today?"

Gill laughed at her.

After a tough few minutes of clambering downwards they arrived at a flat rock at the base of a light waterfall and on the edge of a second, smaller pool. Sandi was already stripping off her clothes.

"You *are* kidding me!" exclaimed Gill.

"Er...no." She was completely naked.

"You'll get hypothermia."

"It's fine. I have a doctor on hand."

"An animal doctor." Gill corrected her.

"I'm just another mammal."

Gill grinned and pulled off her shoes to dangle her feet in, while Sandi dived in, just avoiding the splashes.

"Oh God!" Sandi came up, astonished at the temperature, even though she had known to expect it.

"And *what* a mammal!"

Sandi's figure was just visible in the slightly peaty water.

"This is amazing. I didn't think there *were* any places left like this anymore. That don't have a bloody great car park and a picnic spot next to them with litter bins et al."

"This is just one of several m'dear. But I don't bring anybody here. Ever. You are privileged."

"Yeah, I know," Gill said softly, grinning. "I've been thinking that for a few days now."

"Don't get me started. Oh no, too late." Sandi hauled herself out. "That's about all I can bear. I can do about half an hour in the height of summer. But it's then that you have to be more careful not to be spotted and be reported to the police or country park wardens or some such." She shook herself in an almost canine fashion and took her jumper to sponge off the worst of the water; then flopped down next to Gill, where the rock felt warm to the touch. Sandi pushed her back gently, cradling her head in one hand, so that it was cushioned from the rock.

"Your skin is absolutely freezing."

"But it's tingling, on fire. Warm me up."

Gill rolled her over, the clothed above the unclothed. "Allow me to be your survival blanket, she murmured as she leant down to plant her lips gently on those that awaited her. "Oh God, why do you make me feel so helpless?" She let her mouth travel just above the bare skin down the strong neck and onto the full breasts, still cold to the touch. She breathed warm air onto each of them. Her leg eased its way between Sandi's, propping herself, but gently weighted in the right place and her hand ran down the curved side of her freezing body, feeling its way over the hip bone, through the healthy forest of hair to where she could sandwich it between her leg's weight and Sandi's most secret places. She let her leg lean gently, pushing her fingers inwards. She pulled away gently for air and a whisper.

"My diagnosis is, or will be shortly, according to the temperature I have just taken, pneumonia or hypothermia, if we don't get you off these damp rocks and into your warm clothes soon."

Sandi caught her breath. "Spoilsport."

"Oh no…think of it as unfinished business…and you probably have about a dozen different types of sheep-related bacteria on you." She gave Sandi a gentle kiss and rolled off her, leaving her to pull away reluctantly and find her clothes to fasten them up.

"But I'm immune. From generations of hardy Dales folk."

"But I'm not!"

"Okay. You're probably right. Let's get back to the car. I'm ready for a hot pie or some soup and I know just the place."

"I *love* this. I could do this every day."

"Think of all those other mammals that would miss your diagnosis though."

"Diagnosing *you* is the most fun of all."

Dressed again, Sandi lead the way back up the unmarked path, pulling Gill up when necessary, having the advantage of size and strength. They clambered back to Gill's car and headed over the hill into the next valley, where Sandi had earmarked a cozy pub with a decent homemade menu for lunch. In the afternoon they took a route back that lead them to a traditional cottage now owned by the National Trust, Sandi showing Gill what she could remember from her grandparent's days: the range, clothes wringer and milking stalls. She felt more enthused than she had in a long time discussing her family and soon other branches of the family spilled out, so that Gill was becoming fully informed of the cousins, aunts and uncles, spread over the county and even as far afield as Northumbria, although none in the south, many of whom had shown their support during the 'difficult' years.

By four in the afternoon, they had returned to the cottage, glad to warm up as the cooler night air encroached. Gill ran a deep bath in the upstairs bathroom, which they shared thawing gently together, talking softly, until glasses of wine in hand they returned to the welcoming double bed, to continue their explorations until their energy finally faded and they could sleep, safely in each other's arms.

CHAPTER NINE

History

Sandi had decided abruptly on Sunday morning that it was time to return home. It was usual for her and John to share Sunday lunch and catch up on their news from the past week and plans for the week ahead, she said, and anyway, it 'would be a shame to burst the perfect bubble' by letting Gill realize too much about her 'all in one go', she had added with more than a hint of humor-tinged humility.

After she had dropped Sandi off on Sunday morning and returned home to sort out her house and her head, Gill was very aware that she had fallen immediately and very deeply for this new person in her life. Momentarily she was suspicious of herself. Wasn't it juvenile to fall so instantly into such a deep liking for a person? But it simply did not ring true. Her first impressions had so often been entirely accurate. She was amazed at this woman's sincerity and straightforwardness. Stunned by her own body's empathetic reaction to every instinctively easy, confident movement conveyed by her. Amazed by her easy adeptness at fitting in sympathetically with her environment. Her relaxed, immediate, easy approach to sex! No second-guessing of herself. The way she had dived recklessly, unselfconsciously into the pool and then later had freed a young ram they had passed on the road, asking Gill to pull up the car so that she could untangle the young animal that had trapped itself in the roadside fence with its horns, commenting wryly that she hoped someone would do the same for her flock.

Gill's thoughts continued to orientate themselves towards her new girlfriend as she sorted halfheartedly through a couple of boxes of books. *Girlfriend.* That hadn't been the plan, had it? She asked herself. *No distractions.* But life's not that easy to control. You can't forward plan when it's convenient to bump into someone. When it's the right time to admit people into your life? They just have a tendency to thrust themselves forward unexpectedly. She grinned at the double entendre.

She drifted up to her bedroom and sat down on the stirred up bed sheets. These she would not tidy up or change for a good few days. She flopped back on the bed and stared at the ceiling, allowing thoughts from the preceding two nights to jostle with each other in her head. Sandi in fits of giggles; Sandi with her head thrown back gasping for air. What would the other farmers think if they knew? Not knowing she was echoing Sandi's previous thought path, she found herself retracing her own history.

She'd had only one other female who had reached the status of girlfriend. There had been a crush at school, which was largely unreciprocated and did not count. And she had been such a swot, so determined to succeed and prove herself right and everybody else wrong, that she had not made time for anyone, until Inga had sort of insisted that she made time for *her* at vet school. Gill smiled to herself at her hindsight's interpretation of events. Her ego was forgetting how hungrily she had lapped up Inga's enthusiasm, how they had stolen moments in the slightly prickly hayloft, worked the bars in Edinburgh and enjoyed everything from revising for exams to sea-fishing together. Inga was a dab hand at gutting and preparing any catch, her family having spent summers on the islands off the fjord coast for most of her life, where weeks were spent bathing, relaxing, fishing, getting back to nature. She was blonde, svelte and intelligent. Nothing seemed to bother her, except that she was so intense about everything. At first her motivation and slightly obsessive desire for Gill and herself to be healthy and fit were inspiring, but gradually little digs and hints about Gill's appearance and manner began to grate. It had taken time to see that her enthusiasm was closely related to a tendency to want to control everyone in her life and what they planned to do next, to the point that claustrophobia began to set in and Gill was already feeling herself unable to breathe without permission, even before Inga had surprised her with an invitation verging on insistence that they return to her native country together and make things permanent.

It was a step to be taken apparently without a balanced discussion or a meeting of two minds, let alone two opinions, and at that point Gill had recognized that she was more like a possession than an equal in the relationship. Still, she could see why Inga would need to go home. Leaving her home country forever wasn't Gill's top priority. Inga had suggested that Gill was small-minded and couldn't see beyond her own little world. But wasn't that hypocritical? It was a comment that left her smarting. Perhaps there was some truth there. She wasn't going to be bullied or emotionally blackmailed into someone else's choice. However, when they had parted company and Gill was left licking her wounds, the possibility of a one-year post in Africa had been suggested by her tutor. Although she had to overcome an unexpected nervousness, Inga's jibe had left her wondering at her own courage and anyway, she was intrigued at the prospect. Wouldn't it be an incredible thing to do? It would give her an added string to her bow. The possibility of zoo or safari park work in the future? She discussed it with the tutor and her parents, was interviewed briefly in London and after loading up with an armful of vaccinations and a small library of reference books, she had committed to it.

The suitcase had lain open, looming at her throughout that final night in England before the early flight the next day. In the small, lonely hours of the middle of the night, she wondered what on earth she had agreed to. But by the time she was consumed by the activity of the airport, the excitement of the flight, the warm welcome on arrival and the subsequent glamour of letters and emails to and from home, visits from friends and even parents, and the whirlwind of learning so much helping with animals known only from zoo visits and the printed word, life had taken hold and overwhelmed her former anxiety.

The independent streak in her was made not only more robust and self-sufficient by the experience, but also warmer, friendlier, rounder and more confident. The genuine warmth of the people—wardens, colleagues, locals of many different ethnic backgrounds—often welcoming her into their homes, made her feel accepted and wanted. Although the experience had not been without its dangers either. There had been close shaves with angry, injured animals, poachers, bandits and a snake or two. Enough to humble the arrogant and make any lucky escapee grateful.

She had told herself easily that she had neither the need nor the energy for a personal, private relationship when life was so full and demanding. Many were the mornings that she had slept late beneath her mosquito net because of some nocturnal rescue, poaching scare or woken aching from the previous day's pummeling from the roping or release of some frustrated water buffalo, kudu, elephant or other. It was literally a world away from what she had known before. But even though there were offers to stay longer, she had known all along that the pull of her roots would win and she would be drawn home again.

When Richard, another college friend, had managed to coordinate a dead-cert interview and a post for her at a city practice in York, it had proven to be a likely stepping-stone to link her back again. She hadn't quite foreseen that cats and dogs would be quite so limiting to the imagination after the previous year's opportunities. A bit like Sandi, she had hit the lively night scene in York to compensate. There were ample opportunities in such a buzzing university town. Clubs, restaurants, theatre, strolls down the riverside walks, ghost-tours and the liveliness of students and their professors all enriched the environment. York's city center was compact for any city and still boasted a network of medieval streets, Tudor houses and characterful teashops that would easily compete with Rye or Stratford-Upon-Avon. Gill had danced the night away many a time, when work commitments allowed, with an occasional brief fling or two that never really qualified as a relationship.

A deeper friendship with one of the medical professors at the university had nearly made it into that category. She'd met her at a gay nightclub on a Saturday night, when she'd been out with Richard and some other friends to forget herself after a difficult afternoon fighting and losing the battle for a young Alsatian's life. She had held his head until the lights had gone out in his eyes and it hurt more than usual, the unfairness and randomness of fate. The sophisticated, older woman who had invited her for a drink and a dance, had become a shoulder to cry on that night. They had shared a few afternoons in the park, touring the cathedral and an evening at the theatre, when this professor had accidentally let something slip that made Gill realize she wasn't the only one to be receiving such attentions and that amongst others she was pursuing students. Instinctively monogamous, Gill had given her a piece of her mind, but had been even more taken aback by the attack she received for being so conservative. Anyway, that was the end of it. And it may have been the final straw that motivated her to get out from the world of small minds and small animals to where she felt her talents really lay, the challenges of big shaggy beasts, and apparently the challenges of the wilder country folk who go with them.

She grinned at herself again. Old history already. New pages still to write. What happens next with Sandi? Who calls who? Officially, according to some ancient, unspoken rule of etiquette, because Gill had telephoned to start the ball rolling this weekend, the ball ought to be in Sandi's court. At that moment the telephone shrilled through the house and Gill's heart leapt into her throat. She leaned across to pick up the bedside extension.

"Hi?"

"Gill! Hi! It's Becka. Sorry to bother you."

"No bother. What's up?"

"I'd like to say, come for a game of tennis in the park, but… as it happens we need you to assist at the surgery. Bridget's got a tricky emergency on with one of Marcus's wolfhounds. Daft thing ran in front of a four by four on the estate. We've tried Ethan, but he won't be back from a call at the top of the Dale for another hour or two. Do you mind?"

"Course not. I'll be right over. I was only sorting boxes and I was thinking of coming in to get my reports up to date."

"Brilliant. We're scrubbing up already. Double time for you and there'll be drinks in the pub afterwards."

"I'm on my way."

She hung up. Life goes on. She gathered up her bag and coat, thinking how grateful she was sometimes that her job was such a constant distraction. Not all the time, of course. Twenty-four hours earlier would have been most inconvenient. She chuckled to herself and hurried out of the house.

CHAPTER TEN

A fork in the path

There was a polite knock on the consultation room door followed closely by a head with attitude. Really, it was the hair that had the attitude. Bouncing curls, almost orange in color, framed a cutely cheek-boned pixie face with a provoking smile.

"Are you ready for me?" The elfin face asked.

"Er, yes of course, come in," Gill responded.

"So you are the infamous Gill?"

"I am?" Evidently at a disadvantage, Gill was struggling to recover herself. "I suppose I must be. And you are?"

"Melonie."

"What can I do for you?"

"Well, it's my guinea pig actually. A little off color, not eating her usual food."

"Right. Get the cavey, I mean guinea pig, out please and I'll take a look."

The pale brown, furry mammal was slid reluctantly onto the surgery table, giving a few feeble squeaks of protest as it arrived.

Gill ran her hand over it. "And what's this charming little thing called?"

"Bacon."

Gill spluttered. "Oh really?" She felt around the little mammal's abdomen.

"Yeah, don't want her getting ideas above herself, you see."

"Uh-huh. You know what? Has she been in with any new guineas recently?"

"Yep. My younger cousin looked after her while I had a holiday recently."

"So…the thing is…she's expecting. Pregnant. In the not-so-distant future she'll be a mum."

"Of course! Why on earth didn't I guess that?"

"I'll just give her a few vitamins and you'll need to boost her feed. She's probably just a bit fanciful and feeling a little peculiar. She'll need some peace—solitary—not too much handling and plenty of nesting material, preferably lots of good-quality hay. Perfectly healthy looking otherwise."

"Great. I often use the vet on the other side of Allerdale, Masons, but I was worried he'd be a bit heavy-handed. And anyway, as Sandi's ex, I wanted to meet you."

Gill looked up to meet briefly glaring, accusing eyes, looked away quickly, prodded the guinea pig with the syringe slightly too hard and it squeaked with annoyance. Her brain raced. *Sandi's ex?* Suddenly her heart was doing a tango for one as she completed the vitamin injection.

Her professional veil fell and she felt clumsy. "See? She's absolutely fine. Well there you are." She slid the animal quickly back into its box, deciding not to allow further conversation, and pushed the whole thing towards the client. "She'll be as right as rain and you'll be dealing with mini guineas in no time; about a week I should think. Let us know if you want some more help. Nice to meet you. Becka will sort you in the lobby, I'll ring through and ask her to give you some reading material." She ushered Melonie out before more could be said.

"Do you have any—" Melonie tried.

"Becka will see to everything, I must dash for an emergency calving…" Gill closed the door and leaned against it. *Stalking ex-girlfriends.* Sandi hadn't mentioned that. *Oh my.* A memory of their first meal out at Allerdale came back. She had wondered about Sandi's shifty glances. *How many more might there be?* Gill's heart began to decelerate from its previous pounding high speed. Of course. Of course there would be ex-girlfriends. It wasn't as if her own slate was completely clean. She rang through to Becka and briefed her quickly in a half whisper. But it was only when she put the phone down that a flash of annoyance stung her. On her patch. Tracking her down. Somebody must have said something and then she had come to take a look. Who would have known? Somebody in Allerdale perhaps? She was hit by a brief stab of jealousy or defensiveness or something. *Sandi kissing that little face, running her hands through those corkscrew curls…*

She walked through to the old dispensary, now a small staffroom, bile rising through her, ran a glass of water and rinsed her mouth, spitting disdainfully into the sink. Becka came through as she was gulping back the rest of the glassful.

"You all right?"

"Not completely."

"She's a little minx, that one. She knows perfectly well what she's doing."

"If she books again, don't put her on my sheet. Unless it's an absolute emergency and some creature is dying, please make sure it's with someone else."

"No prob, babes. It's as good as done. I'll put a note on the system. But really…take no notice. Half of the valley knows she can't take no for an answer and that Sandi's been playing dodgeball trying to avoid her."

"And yet I don't know about her…"

"God, I'm sorry. I should have seen it coming. I would have warned you, but she just barged in, saying it was urgent and was prepared to pay the emergency fee. She never comes here usually. I didn't put two and two together fast enough. Thought Ethan might have taken it, but then he took the boxer and then I got so busy I couldn't ring through."

"I'm not blaming you, sweetheart. I just thought Sandi might have mentioned it."

"She probably didn't want to freak you out early on. Melonie can be perfectly charming when she wants to be, it's only later that she can become a little vixen."

"Yes, I've just seen that."

"Come on, let's put the kettle on. She's gone and…" The bell went, calling her attention back to the reception. "Sorry, put three teabags in the pot love," she called as she hurried back to her post.

Gill made the tea, pulled some clean mugs from the cupboard and stared out of the window towards the fells. This is precisely what she had told herself she would *not* get involved with. Some tangled web in a small community that would make working and living a nightmare, where people would take sides and there would be murmuring behind her back and you wouldn't know where to turn next. The solitude of the hills called to her. She should be finished by four and then she could pack a small bag and hike up there away from it all. Ethan was on call and taking the evening surgery with Bridget. The phone shouldn't go. She didn't want the phone to go. Just for once she might leave it behind and be right away from everybody.

Becka clattered back into the room. "Sorry, love. I'll finish those. You're on again. Mrs. Ellis and her cat."

"Thanks." Gill looked at her watch, just an hour to go and she could be free, for the whole weekend if she wanted.

CHAPTER ELEVEN

Hard incline

By four thirty she had left the car in Blackford and was a fair way up the track in decent hiking boots to Winder, the hilltop above the village. She was carrying a small backpack with water and a hastily thrown together picnic tea, first aid kit and a small picnic blanket. She had succumbed to bringing her phone, but had turned it off just for some peace and a chance to think. Her head was buzzing. As she walked, she found herself falling into the rhythm of her steps and the sharp intakes of breath that were necessary to climb the hill.

I'm a fool. Who fell. Fell into the first thing that came along. And I wasn't going to. Now I'm a mess. With a pounding heart. Just because of some stupid ex. And my stupid heart turns over.

Furious with herself, she forced herself into a brisk pace until, by the time she reached the top, she had to double over, gasping to catch her breath. A dog-walker she didn't recognize, who was starting the descent, asked her if she was okay, his face full of concern.

"Fine." She gasped between breaths. "Just…trying…to get…fit." The dog circled her, panting up at her.

"Steady on then," he commented and patted her shoulder with odd, but kind familiarity, then carried on his way, whistling for his dog.

After a few moments, she stood up to turn around, finding the view spread out in all its glory beneath her. The village in miniature, huddled far at the bottom of the slope, with the bakery just in view and the bookshop and surgery noticeable towards the edge of the houses. Beyond that the valley rolled away until it surged up again into the rising Fells that formed the horizon. Shadows changed and moved across the fields as the clouds drifted past, with colors that ranged through blues and purples to greens and browns. She made a mental note to buy a picture that encapsulated that color palette from the mill craft shop, then swigged some water, turned to her right to follow the ridge and pressed onwards.

The exercise was comforting. No longer physically stretched, now on the gentle ups and downs of the fell ridge, she could pace along easily. As the distance and angle changed she caught sight of the mill buildings and her row of cottages tucked into a bank of trees by the river. Sandi might be calling her this evening. She shrugged to herself, convincing herself that she didn't want to speak to her…yet. What other mysteries were there to be unraveled? They barely knew each other really. She had just been going on some gut instinct, when perhaps Sandi's gut instincts were easy to come by. *No, that's unfair.* A little voice spoke inside her.

A fell-runner in some team-colored Lycra ran past and raised a hand in acknowledgement. She smiled automatically at him.

What if Sandi was just embarrassed? And hadn't told her much yet because of some obscure Yorkshire reserve. She wasn't always very forthcoming.

After another forty-five minutes of walking and speculating, she reached The Calf, a peak above the high waterfall Kettle's Spout, found a dry rock and perched herself for her picnic. The distant roar of the waterfall could just be heard above the breeze, even though it was not yet visible over the ridge. Her breathing had settled into the gentle, satisfying depths of light exercise, her blood throbbing happily. The developing evening light was beginning to throw long shadows, with the valley's bowl darkening where the waterfall fell. She had been walking on her own shadow with the light behind her. Munching an energy bar with one hand, she pulled out the local map from her pocket to check her route.

Somewhere in front of her on the lip of the bowl was marked *Stay on the path. Beware sudden cliffs.* She smiled. It was like a message about her life too.

She looked around and agreed with the map. At this point you couldn't see over the lip. You were at the top. At a place where a decision about your route could bring success or disaster. Particularly in the sudden hill fog of low cloud. There were flints and boulders strewn about. The debris of some ancient activity, some other life, as if it could be representative of Sandi's life history. And a path lead away at ten o'clock, with her back to the sun.

She was supposed to walk through the old mess of prehistoric rocks, finding the safe path away from the precipice. The old history and leftovers from Sandi's life. Keep to the track that would lead her, Gill, onwards. Or a track that would lead both of them onwards? Or a track that would lead her away from the precipice, the disaster that might be Sandi? But there was only one path on offer. She examined the map again, tucked away her rubbish into her bag and strode around the summit looking at the ground like a tracking dog. There *was* one more path. It was less well defined both on the ground and the map, where it was marked *Harder route, involves some scrambling.* She grinned at herself. The whole thing was turning into some giant metaphor for her life.

She had always loved being outdoors and exerting herself. Now she could begin to see the addiction for fell-walking. A temporary isolation and delightful loneliness with your thoughts, where the vastness of the wilds reminded you of the comparative insignificance of your own difficulties. Where decisions were needed and respect for immediate danger was a necessity. Perhaps the precipice in this case was not Sandi, but mistaking the danger of Melonie's interference? A sort of misleading path. A red herring. The right path would lead her to beauty and magnificence, in this case Sandi or the waterfall, the wrong path to scrambling through the fog of Melonie's emotional confusion, detouring from the best bit of the journey.

She liked this labyrinthine game. She would take the ten o'clock, northern path and see the waterfall. She shouldered the backpack again and set off, keeping the cliffs away to the right. The path veered away from the edge and after a while crossed over a substantial stream by a well-made sheep bridge. *That must be the waterfall's source*, she thought to herself, liking the idea that she had crossed back into Sandi territory, if the stream represented what was worth having. The path wound round, giving the first views of the opposing cliffs and the increasing roar of the waterfall. She half-expected to see Gandalf appearing on a white horse, the valley was so utterly spectacular and Tolkien in quality. The path began to descend towards the shadows cast by the cliffs with glimpses of the waterfall at various points. A life-giving waterfall bringing water to the valley below it. You could not get too close to it, but it could enhance your life by its presence, you might be able to drink from it at various points, but you couldn't own it. *You can't own it.* From her view across the divide, she could see why she needed to avoid the cliffs. There would be no way down them, perhaps even for an experienced climber with all the ropes that it might entail. Beside them, she could just glimpse a path, more of a sheep-track really, that disappeared into loose scree and reappeared randomly. It looked much more treacherous. She grinned to herself again. She was definitely on the right path. Her feet were heating up inside her boots with the pressure of the descent, but the route was firm and reliable even if it was a little well worn. *Well it would be, because it's tempting and spectacular. And it causes a little discomfort!*

She read the map details. Kettle's Spout. It sounded wonderfully medieval. Magical almost. The highest cascading waterfall in England, falling one hundred and seventy-five meters. It was no Niagara. More of a constant trickle, in comparison, but insistent, persistent, as old as the land itself. The light was fading faster, so she pressed on downwards, without passing another soul; no one since the runner. In the valley floor, with the waterfall fading behind her, now a cheerful, bubbling beck, singing its way over loose shale, she passed a tourist sign explaining the history of some iron-age ruins. Further on, a walled-in field of sheep hemmed the path, clearly in the last stage of pregnancy, brought down to the valley floor for the farmer to keep a watchful eye on. There were a few grumbling protests from the flock at her sudden proximity, despite their safety behind the wall. Again she was faced with a dilemma. The path forked, with a choice to either walk back along the fell slope towards the village, probably a couple of miles through some farmland or back over the more substantial river in the valley bottom towards the road and an inn. She chose the latter, worrying that it was getting too late to retrace her steps if she was to come across any rowdy herds of cows or bullocks on the farmland route. After crossing the river on a delightfully wobbly bridge, she discovered a bus stop with a wait of forty-five minutes for the next bus to the village and stopped in at the inn to kill time.

Unusually, it was a Temperance Inn, run by Quakers, who were incredibly friendly, welcoming her in with choices of where to sit. She opted for the rear garden where, now out of the shadow of the cliffs and fells, the last rays of the evening sun provided some warmth. Not that she needed it too much. She was warm and flushed from her efforts and she realized suddenly, happier and more settled. There was a distant view of the waterfall.

As she waited for her drink, she felt it would be easier to know what to do next now that she had stopped to think, but she might just allow herself a few days breathing space.

CHAPTER TWELVE

The paths converge

"Gill here. Can't answer the phone at the moment. Leave a message!"

"Gill, pick up. Are you avoiding me? I've tried you at work. You blanked me in the street. What the hell's going on? Something's happening and I don't know about it. Are you going to tell me or let everything become impossible and awkward and I won't know whether I can speak to you or not? I'm going to The Hounds tonight. I'll get a booth and keep myself free. Come and see me. Please." Sandi hung up and frowned. She reached for her keys and jacket, heading out of the door into the night to walk the road down to the village.

* * *

Gill sidled into the bar and looked around. She spotted her target hunched over a pint and a newspaper in a far corner. It was true. She had avoided lunch and had ducked down an alley towards the tourist center when she had spotted her further up the street.

Now, this evening, she hadn't been seen yet, and she could leave or stay. But her heart still did a flip at the sight of the tall, gangly figure, so she decided to stick to her former resolve and speak to her. She inched over unnoticed and slid in next to her on the settle.

"Oh, thank the heavens." Sandi lowered the newspaper, breathed a sigh of relief, leaned into her and squeezed her thigh beneath the table. "Where on earth have you been? I thought we had a lunch date yesterday and you just didn't show."

"Yeah, well, I had to do a foaling with Bridget and…I met an old friend of yours. She paid me a visit at the surgery. Unexpectedly. Name of Melonie. Seemed to enjoy teasing me. Turns out Becka said most of the valley know about you and her."

"Oh, shit."

"Exactly."

"She's a pain in the butt."

"I thought so. She'd obviously come in to snoop and have a dig at me, under the cover of some guinea pig trouble or other."

"Not the blessed guinea pigs. Plee-ease. Tell me all."

Gill related her story. The background noise was enough to cover a private conversation without having to shout at each other.

"The thing is, Gill"—Sandi looked long and hard at her—"this gorgeous chick, you by the way, comes into the valley, the Sahara Desert as far as my love life is concerned, and I can't believe my luck. She seems to think I'm worth a second look too and it's like an oasis has appeared over the horizon. After nothing but one camel with an attitude problem…"

"Yeah, I noticed the attitude."

"And I didn't want to tell you about the camel problem, in case, as a vet, you thought you'd picked up some troubled creature with a history of disastrous behavior."

"And have I?"

"I can't speak for myself can I? I did go a bit berserk for a while after me Mam and Dad…Christ, I think you're in for the full confessional…I'd had a crush on a girl at school, a bit of a longer-term friendship at college and I'd kept myself mostly under wraps. Mum suspected and talked to me. She reckoned I'd be best to keep things quiet." She took a long sip from her beer, apparently bracing herself for courage. "It's a church-going community. I used to sit there with her on a Sunday and think it was all balls. We had some old ranty fellow, who thought women in leadership roles and gay relationships were all the work of the devil. Sometimes I'd be seething inside. It's not the same now. Mark, the vicar, he's only been here about three years, he's young and vibrant, not the same shit at all. Not that I go much. But when they were killed, I supposed I sort of lost it for a while. I did go off the rails a bit. Hit the bars in York, met a few strangers and then I realized I was heading for trouble. I pulled the plug on it and threw myself harder into the farm instead. I even got myself tested in case I'd picked up some rubbish or other."

Gill raised an eyebrow at her.

"All clear, thank God."

"Go on…"

"Then out at the pub in Allerdale, one night the farmers had gone there for a change, I met Melonie and well…things developed over a period of time…and she was the first person who really wanted to listen and I drank too much and I cried all over her…and it turned out we had a few things in common. She can be funny and entertaining when she's in the mood, and a jealous bitch at other times. One of those people who doesn't realize that to have a full life you need independence enough to get on with something else sometimes too. I don't mean *be with* someone else at the same time. I've never two-timed anyone. I just mean you have to go off, work, talk to someone else, do other things too, to have a life that's worth sharing."

"Absolutely." Gill had thawed.

"But she became pretty freaky. Needed to know what I was up to. Whether it was raking hay or meeting up with the farmers. And if so, what was every word that had been said."

"Yeah I can imagine that."

"To the stage that she kept appearing unexpectedly, like she was watching me."

"Okay, that's sounding familiar and getting weird. But I still don't know why you didn't say something. I mean, at least to save me from the situation I had to go through. I felt like I didn't know you."

"I thought I'd have a chance to get around to explaining things. How the hell did she get in on it anyway?"

"Who knows? Gossip? Look at us here. We're hardly hiding." Gill cast her eyes around the pub. No one appeared interested, although the barmaid gave a grin as she caught her eye.

"Beth at the bar, Rita at the shop? Who knows? People just get talking. I was on the lookout that night at Allerdale."

"I'm glad you said that. I thought so."

"Transparent aren't I?"

"Not completely. I walked up in the hills for a while afterwards. Trying to work it out."

"Where'd you go?"

"Just Winder and the waterfall."

"You didn't take the sheep track down?"

"I don't think so. It was the path next to the waterfall."

"Good. You need to be a bit careful up there. Somebody fell last year and was killed."

"Oh!"

"Not from the fall either. It was early spring and they were out overnight. Probably the cold finished them off. It can be surprisingly lonely up there. Not many people bother with the full climb up. There's an old story about siren's voices that lure you over the cliffs."

"Well, thankfully I didn't hear those, but it did feel like a strangely mystical place and I sat there doing some thinking."

"Look, I'm really sorry. I should have told you. I didn't want to frighten you off with a psychotic—no she's not that bad—ex, before we'd even had a chance."

Gill grinned at her. A sudden physical urgency reclaiming her. "You're forgiven. Come back with me. Home. I'll find us some ice cream or a bottle of something and…" she paused for thought. "Here, you didn't meet a rather sophisticated professor from the university did you during your mad moments in York? Name of Andrea."

"No, don't think so."

"Thank heavens for that."

"Sounds like you did."

"Er…yes…but nothing much to worry about. I'll save my confessions…but okay I'm not as pure as the driven snow."

"Ooo, do tell!"

"Tell?" Gill grinned. "Come with me and I'll show you."

CHAPTER THIRTEEN

The legend

One afternoon, soon after her first hike to Winder and subsequent reconciliation with Sandi, Gill found herself killing an hour for lunch in Blackford's Old Library building, home to the secondhand bookshop.

She had pulled several likely looking volumes and pamphlets from its musty shelves, ranging from cattle disease to *Local Myths and Legends*. It was in the latter thin volume that she discovered the legend of the Winder Path written down, not just alluded to by Sandi, but actually printed, as if it was more of a fact than a story. She checked her watch. With fifteen minutes before she needed to move herself onto the next call, and genuinely curious, she settled back into the cracked leather armchair to read the slightly faded script.

Over hundreds of years a settlement had developed and fought for its corner in the valley at the foot of the waterfall. It was formed of two circular ditched walls and a cluster of roundhouses within its boundaries. Beyond the walls, on one side, the ground fell away to a sparkling, tumbling stream, that was always pure and never dried up, being fed by the oxygenating waterfall at the head of the valley. On the other side, at a distance were sacrificial bog pits, which were fed to keep the spirits that supplied the waterfall happy. Sacrificial bog pits! Gill thought. How can they know that? The mind reels. But she could feel the legend's descriptions wrapping themselves around her. She continued to read, becoming hungry for the outcome.

On three sides, the village was protected by the steeply rising slopes of the surrounding fells, where their sheep and cattle could graze. In winter the villagers would round them up and bring them to enclosures in the valley. In summer, enough cultivated grains were grown in the fields surrounding the main river to supply the villagers with bread for the year, with grain to spare. In the years of the Roman occupation, the settlement was sufficiently comfortable to be able to increase its wealth by trading animals and breads with the Romans en route to the north and with the other local settlements. Tools, jewelry from the gems thrown up by the sparkling stream and cloths woven from the sheep's wool by clever hands into unique, colorful patterns added to their riches.

It was about this time that the waterfall developed the beginnings of its current name, Catillus, from the Romans, meaning kettle or cauldron, because of the way it spouted out from the top of the hills and poured its way down the cliffs. Fortunately for the village, the Romans were satisfied with trading and a few taxes, largely passing through the valley to more important centers, leaving the villagers free to battle on with their existence. For hundreds of years, the village remained small, but thriving, picking up the innovations that trade and foreign influences brought.

The ambitions of the village chief towards the end of this period of the village history, it was said, were to unite the settlement at the waterfall with its nearest neighbor, to avoid rivalry, resolve old disputes and forge ties, by marrying one of his daughters to the son of the rival village chief.

What a git! Gill was indignant.

Names are lost in the annals of time. Perhaps the chief was called Alric, perhaps the daughter in question was Hilda. However, Hilda had other ideas. Maybe the son in question was unappealing, perhaps she was afraid or did not want to move from her familiar surroundings, but the story goes that following threats and bullying from her father, she crept away from the village in the small hours of the night, climbed the high hills behind the settlement and threw herself off the cliffs to avoid her father's plan.

Gill found herself gulping out loud. She had been standing almost right there. *It's a legend.* A little voice told her somewhere inside her, but a chill seemed to go through her and she shivered, even though she felt quite warm in the comfort of the old building.

From this tragic end, the legend began, that still haunts the cliffs above Kettle's Spout. The dangers of figures or voices, Hilda's presence perhaps, that lures you towards, or perhaps warns you away from, the cliff edge. Depending upon the person or the dilemma.

Whatever actually happened on the cliffs, from that point it appears that the history of the village declined dramatically. It may have been that the feud with the rival village was increased by the sudden snub when the nuptials were cancelled, cutting them off or raiding them repeatedly. None of the ruins that have been found there can be dated into the Middle Ages, whereas the small town of Blackford at the mouth of the neighboring valley, where the road forks to take the valley to the waterfall continued to mature and receive a mention in the Domesday Book. Perhaps Alric lost the trust of his village. Perhaps the two neighboring villages fought or cried their way to their demise. Who knows now?

Gill stood up and smoothed her jumper down, having a vague feeling that she had witnessed an accident or gone through an unexpected ordeal. She gathered up the pile of books, choosing to buy the cattle disease book to read later at home, but returned the *Local Myths and Legends* volume to where she had found it. She tucked it in behind another book, deliberately hiding it, thinking both that she might want to read it again, and also that it was tainted. She shook herself, feeling a little stupid to be behaving in an almost childlike fashion. But a superstitious gloom almost seemed to hang over the shelf, and she turned hurriedly away, to head down the old staircase and back towards the bright, cheerful daylight out in the street.

CHAPTER FOURTEEN

Solving the dilemma

As they lay there, still entangled, Gill murmured, "I've had the most brilliant idea."

"What? Let's do it all again?"

She slapped Sandi lightly on the rear. "No. Fool. A party. Let's get Inga over—oh how she loved a party—and get her to meet Melonie." Gill had been persuaded into describing some of her past. "See? They're a perfect match aren't they? The one a control freak, the other needing to own and be owned completely by somebody. Solves a problem. Inga's been asking to visit."

"She has?"

"Just a bit of general Facebook pestering to everyone."

"I suppose it's kill or cure," Sandi suggested doubtfully.

"Cure."

"One would hope."

* * *

Sandi returned late to the farm. There was no chance to stay out because she was on milking duty. John was still up, feet up on the settle, watching some football. He flicked the screen off as she came in.

"Hello," he began, as Sandi kicked off her shoes, his tone immediately belying some weight on his mind. She knew him too well after all these years. They had cried together, shouted together, shared small triumphs, and laughter too.

"What's up?"

"Should there be something up?"

"Oh don't give me that."

"Fine. What's up is that I'm worried about you."

"Oh. Is *that* all?"

"Yep. That's it. You're sneaking around. What sort of time do you call this?"

"And…you've become me dad now?"

"You know exactly what I mean. I'm just looking out for you. Suddenly…nights away…staying out until all hours. You'll have some accident or other on the machinery…and well, Beth told me she'd seen Melonie in town. Or is somethin' goin' on in York again? I thought you'd left all that behind you. I've had months of you lollopin' around here. Things have changed. *You've* changed. But"—he paused and stared straight at her— "it's not that you're looking unhappy about it."

"Okay." She drew a long breath. "I'll tell you. But don't freak out. And please keep a bit quiet about it for now." She paused for courage. "It's Gillian. The new vet." Anybody who had been in the village for less than half a lifetime qualified as 'new'. "We have a lot in common. I mean *a lot.* I met her the night of Tammy's lambing. Been seeing her ever since."

"Oh…" The sigh escaped him with an obvious sense of release. "That's good. I think." He paused and thought. "That's great…only…she's not going to go buggering off and breaking your heart?"

Sandi smiled. "I don't know. I don't think so."

"You're serious?"

"I might…she looks like she is. C'mon, give us a break, it's early days yet."

"That's a relief. I thought that bloody Melonie was coming back into our lives. Thank God for that. She absolutely pisses me off."

"And Gill, too. She paid her a visit."

"Oh God, that explains it all. That's why she was hanging around?"

"Exactly. We were plotting a party to get her to meet Gill's Norwegian obsessive-compulsive ex and the two of them could hit it off like a pair of fireworks." Sandi laughed to herself.

John liked this, slapped his hand on his thigh and laughed explosively. "And go back to Norway together, never to be seen again. Oh, hell, that's a relief. I'm glad it's not her. And Gill... well, she's all right. I've heard nothing but good reports back. She pulls her weight. The lads have had some decent results."

"Yeah," Sandi repeated quietly, smiling. "Decent reports."

"Want a drink? A Scotch? Go on!"

"Sure."

He went to pour. "It's just that I have something else to discuss." He paused while he sorted out the glasses and handed one over.

"What next? Must be something good. That's the best Glenmorangie."

He drew another long breath. "Well...it's about me. About me and Lisa."

"Oh yeah?" Sandi raised an eyebrow, expectantly. She had half been waiting for this moment. Had mulled it over in her head a few times. What to expect? What to say? Would they demand the farm?

"I want to ask her to marry me."

"What? You haven't already? You're asking *me* first? My God. She'd kill you if she knew."

"No. I don't think so. The thing is. *You* matter, too. She knows that. I've made it perfectly clear to her all the way along. We're family. We're all we've got left to each other. I'm not going to screw it up with you."

"Fuck." Tears had sprung from Sandi's eyes and had started to pour uncontrollably down her cheeks. She took a deep swig from the glass, the best crystal glass.

"Oh, shit," John said quietly.

"Hang on," Sandi gasped and tried to catch her breath. "Give me a sec."

"We won't. I can wait. I can leave it…" he started to gabble.

Sandi stood up and moved over to him, sitting down to give him a massive hug and sob into his shoulder. He threw his arms around her and squeezed her.

"I'm sorry."

"Shut up…you big…ape." She managed between sobs.

He pulled back, waiting for the storm to subside.

"You silly, half-baked eejit. I couldn't be happier for you. I think…" she gasped for breath and wiped her face on her sleeve. John pulled a handkerchief out of his pocket and passed it over.

"It's clean."

"I should bloody well hope so…I think it's the best piece of news since sliced bread and that you are perfect for each other and that nothing would make me happier than some little Johns and Lisas to pass this place onto."

"Thank the heavens. You must understand nobody's booting you out. We've got to find a way to work things out for all of us."

"I should bloody well hope so." Sandi was recovering herself, sniffing. "You boot me out and I'll have the solicitors on your back. However, if I have to listen to the pair of you making the beast with two backs, I will also have the solicitors onto you, so we'll have to think of something." She gave him her best grin. "That's bloody marvelous news. Something to be happy about at last."

"So…I have your blessing?"

"What? We've gone back to the Victorian times? Of course you have you great hairy apeth!"

She squeezed him so hard he cried out in pain.

"I've had some ideas. And one of them is this…" He handed her an envelope.

"What you're serving me notice?"

"Don't be daft."

"Now I'm worried." She opened the envelope. Still sniffing. "What the hell is this?" She waved a headed letter at him, starting to look menacing. "You're buying me out?"

"No. It's not enough for that. And why would I want to do that? I need you. It's from Mum and Dad. Now this is when you can be cross with me…or them. They held back some savings, some insurances, in trust, just in case. Christ…it's like they knew what was coming…or perhaps they just wanted to make our future secure. Look it's not signed just by me."

"Ashleigh and Worth."

"Right."

"And that's not all of it. This is separate to the farm. There's money for both of us and some left over. There was more than we knew. Generations of help. Great-grandpa had his finger in the textile industries."

"I remember hearing stories."

"Yeah…not just stories. Reality."

"But when did you find out?"

"Not long. I went back into everything last week, just starting to work it all out, if I married. Ploughed through the paperwork. I hadn't really paid enough attention. Had to get an appointment to have it fully explained. They put it away to secure our future if we wanted to marry. Like a trust fund. Maybe. You don't have to draw it now. But it might give you choices. Build a separate house somewhere on the farm? Buy in the village? Or *we* can…and leave *you* in here. We can share the farm as ever, it just means rearranging who is here and when, and maybe get in some more help. Expansion ideas…who knows?"

"Blimey."

"Doesn't it turn things upside down?"

"A bit. And everything makes sense too. Mum and Dad. They were such skinflints and we never knew."

"They say you get rich by taking care of your pennies."

"I'll need another Scotch."

"Me too."

Sandi resupplied their glasses, passed his over and stood staring into the amber fluid.

"When are you going to do it? Ask Lisa?"

"As soon as poss. I just needed to run everything by you. Look…" He rummaged in his pocket and pulled out a ring box, flicking it open to reveal a small diamond ring. "Right size, I hope."

"Oh, it's beautiful. Oh hell, I'm off again." Tears threatened to pour, but instead they both laughed at each other.

"You're a soppy date y' know, underneath it all."

"Yeah, I know." She paused, thinking. "But I don't want to move off the farm, John."

"I don't want you to. I thought you might want to have choices, that's all. Just needed to give you the option of freedom."

"This is home to me."

"Good. It's home to *us*. And let it always stay that way."

"When are you going to ask her?"

"I'm going to do it tomorrow."

"Beyond that...I don't want to know!" She grinned, swallowed down the whisky and kissed him on the cheek.

"And the party you're thinking about...could be ours. We'll have a bloody good knees-up. It's about time."

"Congratulations. Mum and Dad would be totally proud of you. But don't mind me. I'm getting off this roller coaster and going to bed. Milking's mine in the morning." Her hands had started to shake, which she recognized as a bad sign. If she didn't take time to calm herself her chest would tighten, she would become short of breath and dizziness would follow. Any abrupt changes to the world around her would start this chain of events she had noticed more recently. She had been wobbly the first morning she had woken up to find Gill had left overnight and then again when Gill had abruptly cut her off when she had not known about Mel. She was furious with herself for her own physical betrayals. She was convinced it wasn't anything physically wrong with her. She felt she should be stronger than this after all she and John had been through in the past.

"Too right. I'm off to get myself a wife in the morning." John interrupted her thoughts.

"Quite right!" Sandi mimicked the crispest of English accents. "Night." And with that, she took herself off to her room, to sit on the edge of her bed, letting her breathing slow down again, in the way that the doctor had once suggested.

CHAPTER FIFTEEN

Another fork in the path

"What's wrong?"

"Nuthin'." Sandi shrugged, refusing to look up.

"Something's up. I know there is. You've gone all quiet on me."

There was a lengthy silence, but Gill waited patiently.

"All right then. Tell me again why you went from Edinburgh to Africa."

"You know this. My course was over, my girlfriend ditched me, I was accused of being narrow-minded and unadventurous, the opportunity arose and I thought I should prove to myself I wasn't."

"And why you went from Africa to York?"

"I missed home. Perhaps I am unadventurous. A job came up in a city with lots of Olde Englishe Charme." She pronounced the 'e's at the end of each word, smiling. "It just seemed right."

Sandi smiled. "And why you went from York to Blackford."

"You know this too. I wanted big hairy beasts again, like you...not just flea treatment and neutering. And...I was accused of being small-minded again. Do you know what? I decided I couldn't give a shit. It's just other people's way of bullying you, emotionally bullying you. And the one thing it did make me realize is that I had to start doing exactly what I wanted to do."

"So you came here. And does it fulfill your dreams?"

"What do you think? It doesn't just fulfill my dreams it fulfills my best fantasies. What's all this about? You want some praise? I can give you praise."

"Oh, it's not that. I'm just afraid of it all being too dull. I'm too dull. I don't want to go anywhere. All I've ever wanted is here in this valley in the surrounding countryside. The big, wide world scares the pants off me. You're a globetrotter."

"Barely."

"I was never that comfortable being away from here. Aberystwyth was necessary rather than exciting. I've been afraid that you'll get itchy feet."

"But I think I've found my home. All I've been wanting is to find somewhere that I don't want to leave."

Sandi gave her a massive hug.

"And if I get itchy feet, which is fairly unlikely, then we'll take some time out *together* and you can come with me to count lemurs in Madagascar or some such mad thing for a fortnight and we'd feel fine because we'd have each other and it would only be very temporary. Frankly if we need a change, a campervan, a week at the Edinburgh Festival or a cozy cottage anywhere would do it for me. We must write it into John's contract with you. A fortnight's holiday to come and do something crazy with Gill." She stroked Sandi's cheek. "Anyway, you can show me some mad things. You do show me mad things! I want to swim with the dolphins like you and strip naked in remote pools."

"Ah, that I *can* arrange. It's a deal. But…I want to. I mean, I want to do something mad while the sap is up around here. Before it all settles down into a regular routine again. Take me somewhere. I'll be confident with you."

"Okay…if you're sure."

"Yes."

"Then leave it with me."

CHAPTER SIXTEEN

Mud on the track

It had been some weeks since Bridget had taken her to one side. She had called Gill into her consultation room when surgery had finished and the clients had all departed. This wasn't something that usually happened and Gill had found herself going over the previous few days for possible criticisms that might be coming her way.

However the conversation had opened well. Bridget was pleased with her work, but more than that, she was delighted with the feedback that was coming in. Even some of the tougher characters had softened and given her praise for her thoroughness and dexterity with the animals.

Bridget talked around in circles for a while, ever decreasingly coming in towards the aim, her target.

"The thing is…"

Oh, here it comes, Gill thought.

"…well, it's come to my notice…has been brought to my notice…that you have become rather close to one of our clients, the Heltons, long-standing clients, who are valuable customers to us."

Right Bridget. Where's this going? "Meaning…Sandi?"

"Exactly. Sandi." There was a lengthy pause, while Bridget chose her next words. "I would just like you to know that, not only are they valuable clients to the practice, but also friends. We were all devastated by what happened to their parents, Jack and Lillian. It shook the village and we all became guardians to them. Not that they really need much help, as it has turned out. They are very capable."

"Yes, I get that impression."

"Quite."

Crunch time. Bridget—prude or liberal?

"So I'm correct in thinking you've been seeing Sandi?" Bridget continued.

More of her than you would care to imagine. "That would be right."

"Well, I'm glad that's out in the open. I just want you to know that that girl is pure gold dust and that I would like to see you taking care of her and making sure things work out okay. If anybody could do that girl some good it would be someone like you and not…" she paused. Gill found she was breathing more easily after apparently holding her breath, but Bridget continued, "a gossip and troublemaker like Melonie Brooks who rather enjoyed trying to stir it up with me and incidentally, nearly accused you of being heavy-handed with her cavey, which I would like you to know I did not give her the time of day with. Not least because her reputation precedes her."

"Oh, help." Gill had leant on the counter. "The last thing I wanted in coming here was to get tangled up in something."

"And I can well believe you. And…if I were that way inclined myself I can see why someone's head would be turned by Sandi Helton. However, can I just ask you to do two things please?"

"Of course. Fire away."

"Firstly, please be a bit discreet. We have a few old stick-in-the-muds around here, who are worth something to us in the practice. But you don't need to worry about them too much. Villagers tend to accept a *fait accompli* as long as they aren't confronted directly. And as I said, the Heltons have a special place in our hearts. Secondly, for goodness sake make Sandi confront Melonie and sort this all out before it gets any worse."

"Right. Thanks, Bridget."

"Thanks?"

"Just that. Thank you. For being so down-to-earth."

"Ah, that would be my role in this practice. Mother Earth. Like the Celtic Brijit of time long ago."

"Now you're starting to lose me."

"You've got some reading to do girl. Catch up on the local legends. There's a whole wealth of superstition that still makes this place tick."

"Funny you should mention it. I've been noting that myself."

"Right. See you later. Must get on with preparing these spreadsheets for Alan."

And with that, a tricky corner had been quickly and deftly negotiated again by Bridget. Gill had to admire her diplomatic abilities. She could imagine the confrontation with Melonie and Bridget's unruffled, placid response.

But really! Sandi would have to do something about this. With the woman now trying to *criticize* her to her boss?

CHAPTER SEVENTEEN

Coffee break

"So here's the thing…" Sandi stirred her coffee thoughtfully, letting the foaming top be drawn down into a spiraling vortex inside the cup. She was sitting opposite Melonie, at Gill's behest, on a Saturday morning in a small café in Allerdale. Melonie had agreed to meet her, eagerly and perhaps a little surprisingly given the recent turn of events. Melonie had ordered a tall hot chocolate topped off with a peak of cream and was dipping a large marshmallow into it. *Is that supposed to be seductive?* Sandi wondered as she paused to formulate her next sentence. Mel had not exactly tried hard with her outfit, just jeans and an un-ironed shirt, which could be either a good sign—that she was past caring, or a bad sign—that she was overly preoccupied with her thoughts.

"The thing is…" Sandi continued, "I know it's all a bit awkward. That, we…y'know…and then…other stuff's happening now…" *That wasn't a good start.* Sandi tried to recover herself. Mel was just staring at her with enormous eyes and dunking her marshmallow. "What I'm trying to say is…"

What I'm trying to say is leave the hell alone Mel! "…is that I'd like to invite you to a party."

"Party?" Melonie echoed distractedly. This wasn't quite what she had been expecting.

"Yep. John's having a bash. Blackford Hall. And…well I know it's been tough…breakin' up…and all…and it would be good if we could stay friendly like and there'll be dancin' and lots of people coming…it should be a laugh. Let's try and put some water under the bridge and perhaps…" she looked at Mel pointedly, "…p'raps we can stop pokin' around in each other's business, like stirring things up at Redbridge's."

Melonie had enough good grace about her to look down into her drink and mumble, "Er…you heard…maybe I'm sorry about that."

"Right. Exactly. Come along on the twenty-fourth and have a right good time and I'll buy you a drink and introduce you to some of the others."

"All right. Sounds like an idea. I've been thinking so much about those evenings we had."

"Mel, there were three of them."

"Yes, I know," she said pointedly, looking up with a hard spark in her eyes, but catching herself added more softly, "I remember. But I also know what you said last time and I can't help it if I'm finding it hard to let go and just forget it."

"That's the point though. I don't think you should forget it. Stuff that happens. It happens. It doesn't mean you have to forget it. You were there for me…" Sandi gritted her teeth internally. She had gone through this in preparation with Gill. So far so good, "…when I really needed you to talk to."

"Yeah, that was a tough time for you."

"Yep. And you were the one who took the time to listen and help. And I don't forget that. I'm thankful. To you. And to everyone who helped us through. And that's why I don't want things to get awkward. God knows, I'm a rough diamond and it's getting pretty tiring having to talk about 'feelings' to anyone. I'm rubbish at it. So what I suggest is that we eat cake and be merry." She stuck her fork decisively into a large slice of homemade chocolate cake, keeping the other hand that was starting to tremble tucked firmly under her leg. "And I'll pay."

She then sat and patiently listened to Mel's memories of the two of them and what it had meant to her, passing her a napkin when she became tearful and patting her platonically on the arm. Together with Gill, they had worked out a possible way forward: that it would be better to allow Mel to feel valued than to decimate her, that most of her behavior was because everything was spiraling out of her control. If Sandi could find it in herself to be supportive and navigate the ship into calmer waters, the effort would pay off.

It seemed to be working. Sandi had already had her moment of fury at Mel, storming around Gill's cottage when the news had been relayed to her, fuming at Mel's interference and her own neediness to have become entangled with her in the first place. *The bitch has the nerve to make crap for you at work* had been her precise words.

Still, she should bite her tongue. Her own behavior had not been perfect. Her own use of Melonie was as distasteful to her as Mel's behavior had been at Redbridge's. She needed to salvage something from the wreckage for the sake of both of their self-preservations. And after all, her new-found adventure meant she had enough constructive emotion inside her to be generous.

By the end of their coffee shop appointment, they parted on better terms than they began and Mel's reiteration of some type of an apology and a wistful smile as Sandi braved a hug were indicators that the future might be more constructive.

Sandi's hands were shaking only a little as she drove away.

CHAPTER EIGHTEEN

Vaccinations

"It's good of you to give up your day off for this," John called across, as he manhandled the next sheep through.

"No problem, it's nice to meet you all properly, and anyway any day with animals is a good day in my book. It was in the diary, so it just seemed to make sense to tie my visit for lunch in."

He grinned across at Gill, nodding at the cacophony of ewes. "What, even these bad-tempered mares today?"

Sandi clanged the gate shut decisively. "Well, it's not exactly a day off now is it?"

"Not exactly." Gill continued to inject the lambs. They were penned in for marking. The worried ewes were bawling at them from a nearby field. Three of the Heltons' sheepdogs were slinking around waiting for some action. Gill's new Jack Russell, Charlie, named for his tendency to act up and still be silly, observed it all patiently from on top of a bale of last year's straw, tied up on a short lead. "However, being invited to lunch certainly makes up for that."

"Ay, and you'll like Lisa's lunch," remarked John.

"Hey, not just Lisa's lunch. I slaved over the dessert before coming out here." Sandi pointed out, calling from her position by the far gate, where she was sorting the lambs through from one pen to the larger holding pen. She tucked one under her arm and headed over to the field, calling back. "This one's done and mother's doing her nut."

Frank Harris from the village was up to help, loping along with his tall frame and experienced touch. He was about forty, Gill guessed, and she had heard how he had been a godsend to them all. His dad's own smallholding had gone under in the last recession and he had been trying to make a living with painting and decorating since then, keeping his own three sons and wife, until the Helton's bereavement. He had appeared voluntarily, leaning on a fence one day, watching the shearing that year and with a quiet, "Need a hand?" had since become a regular and indispensable feature at the farm, now fully paid up in employment and working a five-day week for them, often bringing his eldest son along for work experience. He called the dogs across to lie down, while he ferried the penultimate batch of lambs through to the field.

Gill stood up and straightened her back out, with a few clicks, dropping the last of the empty phials into the carton at the top of her bag.

"That's it then," John called, closing the gate behind him, following the last of the animals through the pen to walk behind them to the field. "C'mon you daft things."

Gill untied her heavy overalls and packed away the syringes. She watched the others walk the lambs through and gate them in, then stop to lean on the fence and look as the animals re-sorted themselves into their families with considerable fuss and bleating, before heading off away from the farmyard. Frank called the dogs back, one of whom bounded over the gate at full pelt and the other two slunk more gracefully under the fence where there was a slight dip. It looked as though John was pointing out the gap to Frank, perhaps highlighting a repair, making sure the lambs couldn't do that trick too. Gill closed her bag and went over to Charlie to free him. He yapped at her happily and stood on his back legs. "All right." She said, before untying him. He leapt off the bale and suddenly, the sheepdogs, now off duty as it were, bounded over apparently like any other pet dogs to run rings round each other and greet the new arrival. Charlie was caught up in a high-spirited frenzy for a while, until John yelled over to stop the din, causing the dogs to slink around again, but still playfully nosing and rolling with each other. She washed her hands thoroughly on the outside tap, knowing she would do so again inside the house, then loaded her bag and overalls into the car.

Unexpectedly, an arm was around her shoulders, and a light kiss was placed on her ear. "No escape. You have to come to lunch. Lisa's expecting to meet you," Sandi teased.

"Why would I want to escape? I'm starving."

"The in-laws-to-be are here. They're very nice."

"Oh, okay. Fine. Er…do we have to be on best behavior?"

"I doubt it." Sandi grinned at her. "John thinks you're great by the way. He said that was the easiest marking session he's ever had and Frank said 'Ah've never seen it done with so little fuss,' which is praise indeed all round." Sandi tied up the collies. "Come on. Let's go."

"And Charlie?"

"He can come in. We can let him out from time to time."

They headed over to the house where delicious smells of a roast and apple pie were drifting out to meet them. Inside, everyone was seated already at the large, scrubbed kitchen table. While they went to wash themselves with muffled giggling from the hall bathroom, Lisa and John dished up the meal, so that when they returned plates had been loaded with steaming roast potatoes, garnished with rosemary, roast beef, Yorkshire pudding, rich gravy and a variety of vegetables had been passed around. Charlie had settled himself by the fireplace.

Conversation was lively ranging through wedding paraphernalia and party preparations to farm and livestock talk. Gill questioned John over his decision to vaccinate rather than dip their flock. It turned out that there had been very little trouble with flies and ticks on the Helton fields and the preference was also to preserve the environment by not adding to the load of organophosphates to be tipped or wasted at the end of the process. Why shouldn't you break with tradition, if technology and science had moved on to provide safer, cleaner ways to provide the same result? This was John's opinion, chiming precisely with her own.

Lisa's parents were easy-going, her mum having a delightfully ribald sense of humor, laced with her lyrical Scottish accent and a chuckling laugh. She was happy for Sandi that she was getting to see so much of another young lady her age, she said, eyeing Gill with a wink. Sandi colored up as the thought flitted across her mind about just how much she had seen, provoking a sympathetic twang from her lower abdomen.

The party date and venue had been settled, a band, barn dancing and a traditional 'bring a dish and a bottle as a contribution' approach had been taken, although with allocation of courses and styles of food being organized amongst their friends by Lisa and her mother.

As a natural lull occurred before dessert, Sandi suggested to Gill that they should let Charlie go out and mix with the dogs. Outside the sun had gained in strength and burst through the clouds, warming the afternoon. The dogs were not immediately visible, until they traced their long tethers into one of the open hay barns, where the four of them were piled happily together, exhausted from their earlier frolics, on a lower tier of bales, the oldest dog Sam below them on ground level. Charlie jumped up to join them. They went inside to fondle them around the ears, clucking at them affectionately, and as they turned to head back Sandi pulled on Gill's hand and pinned her against the warm wooden wall inside the barn, her pelvis pushed firmly against Gill's. Her hand brushed the hair back from her sweet face. She looked deeply into the eyes that questioned her gently and inched forwards until her lips met those she was seeking with softness and intensity both at once. She pulled back and looked again.

"I think...I've fallen in love with you," she said quietly, simply, and shrugged slightly self-deprecatingly. She waited a moment, her eyes searching over Gill's checked shirt for an answer.

It was not long in coming and she looked up into her face again as the response came.

"I know I have already." Gill spoke softly and leaned in to confirm it with her lips, which were met with a warmth that ignited her in the most secret places of herself.

"Oh help, I want to do something about it right now."

"But instead we need to go and be good company and sample your apple pie!"

"Right. But the first dance is mine at the party. Okay?"

"My card is marked." Gill smiled and pulled Sandi away from the wall. "Come on now." Charlie followed them back reluctantly.

"Is Inga really going to come over for the party then? She said yes?"

They headed back towards the house.

"Absolutely. She said she'd love it. She'd been planning to make a trip back to 'my old stomping ground'." Gill mimicked a Scandinavian accent poorly.

"And not just to see you then?" Sandi asked tentatively.

"She and I? We both know that ship sailed. She hasn't been backward in coming forward about a fling or too since then. I'll show you her Facebook page some time."

Sandi gave an audible sigh of relief and Gill gave her a playful peck on the cheek.

The marking of the card would have to wait. Gill only had a little time to imagine being swung around the dance floor by Sandi, as the calls came from the farmhouse for dessert, which turned out to be delicious and then, almost immediately, John invited her out to see the prize ram, the dogs slinking around their ankles at the promise of an adventure. Sandi stayed back to help clear up, leaving them to get to know each other.

All in all, Gill mused, a very satisfactory outcome to the day.

CHAPTER NINETEEN

Barn dance

Inside the village hall, the band was at full throttle. A piano accordion, two violins, string bass, flute, drums and the dance caller had stirred up the atmosphere, with so many bodies heaving themselves in tempo around the room that the temperature was starting to raise the roof. A Circassian Circle had been in full progress.

"Walk out…" came the call over the sound system, above the relentless, bubbling rhythms of the band, "Swing…and… promenade…" The caller's voice, although only spoken, was rhythmic and melodious.

The circumference of bodies was nearing the end of this particular effort, red faces and dewed brows indicative of their prolonged efforts. As the band slowed, drawing to its final cadence, there was a massed sigh of relief and laughter.

"And bow. Thank you, everybody. We're taking a ten-minute break to catch our breaths and a pint. See you all shortly for A Dashing White Sergeant. Circles of six please. Think about that!"

Gill watched Inga and Melonie return to the table, laughing and breathless as each fell into an empty chair.

"Bravo!" Gill complimented above the background din.

"Oh, my! You Brits know how to be…silly," Inga gasped.

"Yep! Here come the beers."

Sandi arrived, placing down a loaded tray with some care. The two newly arrived dancers dived in with gratitude. Gill noticed with some relief that Mel's eyes barely dwelt on Sandi at all, no more than standard politeness called for.

"Somebody's goin' ter have a heart attack before the evening's out," Sandi stated, pointedly sinking into a broad vernacular. "Yer should see the red faces at the bar."

"At least you have some medics on hand." Gill indicated the practice doctors, relaxing at the corner of the bar. "They would prescribe this as good exercise, wouldn't they?"

"Maybe, but p'raps not mixed with the beer!"

"I don't know. Beer is nearly as old as the human history of this place, and still the human race survives."

"Yep, I always thought there's something medicinal in the peat water."

John and Lisa were recovering at the other end of the largest table, surrounded by friends and Lisa's family. John gave them a wave from the head of the table and raised his glass with a massive grin, which began another round of glass raising and general cheering that spread down the table and round the room.

Men who were willing to dance were in shorter supply than the women, or at least they were rotating themselves out from the bar on a more random basis, which meant that there were multiple all-female pairs being spun around the room, from children to the elderly. Becka appeared and claimed Inga for the next dance. Gill already had her card marked by Andrew from Meadow Farm, which left Sandi to do the right thing and take Melonie around the floor.

Inga had proved herself to be unexpectedly good value. Although inexperienced at 'the barn dance' she confessed, her free time at Edinburgh had not been wasted and most of her dance moves learned at Scottish ceilidhs were serving her well, enabling a certain abandoned enjoyment of the throbbing music and pulsating rhythms to burst forth from her in gales of laughter. She and Gill had caught up with each other happily, with no hint of any former rivalry and even satisfactory concessions on Inga's part that she had turned out to be less adventurous than Gill. As Sandi spun Mel reluctantly around the dance floor, she noticed Mel's attention wandered repeatedly to Inga's gay abandon and finally when caught in the process towards the end of the circle, Mel managed a sheepish grin at Sandi.

Eager to capitalize on the turn of events, as the sergeant drew to his close, and many were still bent double, with their hands on their knees or their hearts, some gasping for breath, Sandi moved quickly to cut in on Becka and Inga who were still giggling breathlessly, and do a partner swap. This meant that Becka was happily hurled around in the ensuing dance by a much chirpier Sandi, and Inga was partnered by the newly blossoming Mel. The hint of contrivance or perhaps best described as a touch of favorably manufactured circumstances seemed to be working.

The third dance in the sequence, for those who stayed the course, evolved at a more sedate pace with arches and genteel promenading, by which stage partners had swapped again, enabling Sandi to be partnered with Gill finally, Becka to be escorted by Andrew and a still giggly Inga to be stationed with an increasingly admiring Mel. Sandi couldn't help but raise an eyebrow in comical fashion, rolling her eyes and managing a quick word in passing to Gill to indicate the outcome. "Bingo!"

When this dance drove home to its conclusion, it was noticeable that all parties did not immediately return to their communal table. Andrew and Becka drifted off to the bar, Inga and Mel headed out to the hall's back garden for a breath of air and Sandi marched Gill off in the opposite direction towards the front of the hall and the High Street entrance.

"You're being purposeful..." Gill managed above the background din as they headed out into the corridor.

"Damn right," Sandi replied and then took an abrupt right turn. Throwing open a door, and after a brief glance within, dragging Gill inside and closing the door abruptly behind them. The noise from the hall was immediately muffled, both by the closed door and the muted-effect brought on by a sudden assault on their nostrils of faded bleach. It was pitch black.

"Broom cupboard?" Gill managed.

"Uh-huh," Sandi grunted.

"How romantic!"

Hidden from the bustle outside, and left only to feel her way, save a small slither of light from beneath the door, Gill's heart rate leapt at Sandi's urgent kisses. The darkness served only to highlight the effect and the odor of cleaning products would never mean quite the same thing again.

Sandi pulled away. "Enough already."

"No, not enough," Gill murmured.

"No, quite. Not enough. But I won't be able to walk out of here with a straight face in a minute."

"You need a straight face?"

"Actually, no, I don't."

"Exactly. However, I won't be able to walk at all, if we don't postpone this."

"Oh, how I like the word postpone at this very moment. Oh, my God. I am going to wet myself with excitement in the waiting."

"What a vision!"

"Your place or mine then?"

"Oh, I'd recommend mine," suggested Gill, "that is, if it works for you. Won't you have half the village descending on yours tonight?"

"Lord knows. Oh, hell, d'you think I'll have to show up?"

"No. Surely not. Not if you show now and get out of this cupboard. Go and be very public and make that speech or something."

"Actually, I am supposed to do that."

"Right. Go and get it over with."

"Will you check me over before I have to go and present myself."

"Darling, I'll *always* check you over."

"Very funny. Let's get it over with then. Out of the closet." And then realizing what she was saying, they both dissolved into hysterics.

It would have been a very peculiar sight to see for anyone who happened to witness the two grown women stepping out of a broom cupboard, crying with laughter, faces flushed and their clothing slightly in disarray.

It took them more than a few moments to calm down and stand upright. Then, as Sandi tucked herself back in, Gill made a few inspection turns around her, and after a quick splash of cold water in the Ladies' loo to return their complexions to a more satisfactory color, they wandered back into the hall.

Becka intercepted them almost immediately, as if she had been looking for them.

"It's working! Mel and Inga—they've been out in the back garden—all '*oh what a beautiful night*' and stargazing. Andrew and I were out there grabbing a quick breath of air and I practically had to make him duck behind the bushes, so as not to interrupt their moment."

"Ooo…Andrew and I!" Sandi teased.

Becka colored up. "Yeah…and? Anyway where have you two been lurking?"

It was Gill's turn to blush. Sandi chuckled.

"Never mind," Becka continued. "Bingo! Full house! There was talk of reciprocal trips to Norway and walks over the hills. See what I mean? We couldn't have hoped for more. No more '*Oh Sandi*'." Becka delivered this with large puppy-eyes.

"Let's hope so for all our sakes." Sandi agreed.

"Anyway, just thought I'd let you know. I'm off to get Andrew a drink." She delivered this with a comical wink and disappeared back towards the bar.

Gill felt Sandi squeeze her hand and heard a satisfied sigh escape her.

A lull in the proceedings had ensued, so after a word with her brother, Sandi took to the small stage and the microphone, clattering her beer glass with a teaspoon to attract attention.

The noise level subsided to a murmur and faces from all over the hall turned towards her, people drifted back from the garden or outlying banquet rooms to listen.

"Right...well..." she began tentatively, "it's not my usual line of work t'make speeches, as yer know. I'm better off with sheep and cattle than people." This raised a sympathetic laugh, which gave Sandi courage to continue. "First, I want to say thank you t'yer all, for being here, not just to celebrate my brother's engagement to this very lovely lady, Lisa, who we have all known and loved for a long time..." This raised a small cheer.

"But also...sheesh, I promised meself I wasn't goin' to well up..." But she had to pause briefly and wipe one eye with her sleeve, taking a mouthful of beer to encourage herself. "...but also, I want to thank you all for your support these past years, since we lost our folks. It hasn't always been an easy time..." A hush had settled on the audience, "...because, well, Mam and Dad they were good folks who worked hard." At this point there was an 'aye' or two in agreement from the crowd and a few 'here, here's'. "And John an' I have had to learn fast. But I really thank you all for everythin' you've done to help us with that. We couldn't have managed without your advice, contributions, friendship, hard work and sometimes shoulders to cry on." She managed to pick Mel out of the audience and give her a shrug and a smile. "I don't want to mention you by names, because I'd be here all night trying to remember everyone and being afraid of having left someone out. But anything you've ever done, from major things like helping out at lambing and shearing, to the smaller things like a friendly smile or a hello, have all made a difference. And well now, here we are, wishing my brother John and Lisa a good future together and a new chapter in our family history. And I know that Mam and Dad would have been really pleased for you both. And really proud of you. And would know that the future of our farm and our little contribution to the future of our village and the countryside around here was going to be safe with you, and with me too. I'll still be a part of things! You're not getting rid of me that easily!" There was a laugh at this and John yelled out, 'Blast—naw, I'm only jokin', who'd want to get rid of you?' Which continued the laughter.

"Okay, someone help me out here, I'm not going to last much longer." To which there was scraping of chairs as John and his father-in-law-to-be headed towards the stage in rescue, "...just to say I'm lookin' forward to welcoming Lisa into our family and thanks again to all of you, friends old," she gestured towards Frank, who heckled her with 'hey, less of the old', "...and new." She looked to Gill, who unashamedly blew her a kiss, "...and long may the merriment continue!" To which there was a rousing shout and applause, as John arrived at the platform, gave her a huge hug and a kiss and playfully wrestled the microphone from her grasp. It was only then that she realized she had been gripping it so hard that her fingers had nearly seized around it.

"Bless your heart, Sandi. It's a good one. Now I have the difficult task of topping what my little sis' said..." and off he went to do so, while Sandi moved back into the crowd, her eyes starting to blur with the pats she received on her shoulders, the squeezes of hands on hers and kisses and hugs pressed upon her. She managed to find Lisa while her brother spoke and wrapped her in a hug, whispering, "I mean it. I'm so pleased for you both." And pull herself gently away with dignity, her eyes starting to spill with the unexpected tears, she wasn't sure why, perhaps memories of her parents, perhaps one of those moments when the junction of change in the path of your life seems so strange and unbearably both pleasant and odd at the same time. Until a firmer, familiar-sized hand squeezed hers and the jolt of familiarity gave her a tad more strength and self-control.

"Bravo," Gill whispered in her ear. "Brilliant." And Sandi managed a smile, coping with a few more friendly jokes and comments towards herself as the speeches continued for another five minutes.

Once John had returned from the stage, she hugged him and slapped him playfully on the back, then after a moment's whispering and a final conspiratorial smile with each other, she approached Gill again.

"C'mon, let's go now."

"Really?"

"I've cleared it."

"Give me a sec." Gill went to say a farewell to the vet's crowd, who were now propping up the bar with the doctor's crowd, and then they were free to leave. And in a moment, after retrieving bags and jackets, they were out into the crisp, reviving air of High Street, to walk the half mile or so down to the mill.

The night became still as the racket from the hall subsided behind them, until they were left with the click of their heels on the pavement. The trees rustled overhead, a gentle breeze stirring their new leaves, the clarity of the star-speckled sky beyond.

"It's so clear this evening."

"Mmm. The start of beautiful things."

Sandi put her arm around Gill's shoulders, resting it lightly as they walked, their pace decreasing, suddenly the hurry to get away from the public face of the world fading with the end of the street lighting of Blackford.

"Look at the hills," Sandi murmured.

"I know. Are they menacing or comforting? I'm not sure."

"Both. Fierce in their total disregard for humankind, but safe because they never change, and if you respect them, they keep everything the same. Full of paths."

"That was a lovely thing to say. It took me a while to understand that when I first got here."

"Come here." Sandi steered Gill gently off the pavement, through a gap in the stonewall.

"Mind your step," she added, as they followed an earth path through the undergrowth down to a small beach beside the river, where the water chuckled its way underneath the road bridge. The moonlight caught the waves and rivulets through the rocks and stones, but the beach was substantial, heaped with debris, churned up and laid down by the floods. She patted a large rock for Gill to come and perch.

"Me and John. We used to come here as kids sometimes. You can sunbathe and swim in summertime. As long as you're careful, the central current's strong enough to sweep you away after it's rained."

"Sounds fun. Apart from being swept away."

"Aye there's an occasional incident, when the kids get things wrong. There's usually a rope swing, tho' I can't see one at the moment."

Sandi swung her legs over and around so that she encircled Gill and could hold her from behind, resting her chin on Gill's shoulder. She kissed her briefly on the neck.

"That comfortable?"

"Fine." Gill had a sense of something significant, an important moment pending.

Something scurried in the undergrowth behind them, causing Gill to startle. "What was that? A fox? A badger?"

"Naw. Not big enough. Weasel maybe?"

Gill felt a shiver go through her. "Gosh, I'm cold suddenly."

Sandi hugged her and then disengaging, she hauled herself around and leant Gill a hand to climb down. The moment had passed.

"Let's go then."

"Warm up under the duvet?"

"Sounds good." Sandi took her hand and squeezed it gently, leading the way back up the path. They took a brisk pace now and headed along the country road, the pavement petering out as they passed the marker for the boundary of Blackford Village. Sandi pulled a small, but brilliant torch from her pocket and lit the road a few paces in front of them. It was still a surprise to Gill that the countryside at night could be so dark, the shadows so light-absorbingly matt black as to be mildly threatening. She'd known it in Africa, of course, where the threat wasn't even mild sometimes, and an outlying camp could be startled awake at night by the snort of hippos or the clatter of some curious creature investigating the saucepans. But usually, there would be a campfire left burning, leaving comforting firelight dancing on the canvas. She linked her arm through Sandi's. There was hardly any traffic, just the occasional car, briefly breaking the silence with a sudden explosive appearance of light and engine noise. Now, the houses of Blackford were behind them and the next cluster of cottages would be at the mill.

They were both mildly intoxicated from the party and the peaceful happiness that found them alone, undisturbed, their footsteps falling into synchronization, a country-dweller's lolloping, persistent pacing.

"Barn owl!" Sandi flicked her torch ahead to catch the ghostly white wings disappearing over the hedgerow.

"Magical," Gill echoed.

"Okay. What I was trying to pluck up the courage to say is…y'know by the river…is that, well, I'm not sure what to do. I'm a bit scared."

Gill stopped, halting their progress and looked hard at her companion. "Of what?"

"Not you. You ninny."

"Good."

"No. Of what to do. So, y'know, John passed this inheritance money on to me, a portion of the estate, but not everything. And I'm thinking, how do I play this out? I hate junctions. Decisions. Where I can't see where they'll take me. How d'you know which one to choose? What to do? Should I give them my blessing to live in the farmhouse? I mean it's always been my home too. Do I buy something? Or convert a barn? Live in, live out? It's doing my head in."

Gill couldn't help but laugh at the delivery of this speech and in particular the last line. She stopped herself as she saw Sandi's confused, puzzled expression.

"Sorry. I know it must be a weird time for you."

"Yeah, exactly."

"It's not what you said, it's the way that you said it." She pulled on Sandi's hand to get her moving again. "C'mon, I think better when I'm moving."

"It wasn't *me* that stopped us."

"I know. I also know it's a big decision and a fork in your path. But, think about it, the farm, the daily workload is going to carry on being and evolving as it ever has done. All you need to decide is the where. Where do you want to wake up in the morning or lay your head at the end of the day?"

"That's easy. Next to yours."

Gill stopped again. But restarted herself after just a missed beat in the rhythm of their walking. Sandi, who had continued on in that missed beat, turned back to face her and pulled her onward.

"Is that okay? I mean I don't want to come on too strong?"

"Oh, my God, come as hard as you like."

"Oh hell! You've done it again."

"Done what?" Gill was giggling.

Sandi pulled her off the main road down a side-walled path, beside a gate into an empty field. She let go of her hand and brushed around with her torch.

"What *are* you doing? You mad thing," Gill asked.

"Checking for nettles."

"Why?"

"I don't want to sting your bum, or mine."

"What?" Gill barely managed the word before Sandi's mouth had pressed onto hers and she had pushed her down onto what must have been an old bench against the drystone wall, hidden from the road.

"It's a bit cold."

"I'm not cold…here have this…" Sandi wriggled herself out of her heavy leather jacket and swung it around behind Gill and over her shoulders, "Can't you wait another couple of hundred yards?"

"Not really…" and she had crouched down in some way or other, switching the torch off, so that darkness surrounded them apart from the stars in the sky and a hint of moonlight. Gill dropped her bag somewhere onto the ground and found herself sinking into the moment, the silence of the night and the darkness, Sandi just a shadow of warmth, gentle but urgent lips suddenly on hers, hands finding their way again over her body through her shirt and skirt. The game was a mysterious game of touch. A hide-and-seek of sensation in the inky blackness. And Sandi was so hot. Hot enough to heat the two of them, her hands like a furnace as they threaded their way to caress her breast and harden her nipples, to ease their way between fabric and skin until skin could be touched by skin exactly where it was needed most.

"Aah!" A sigh escaped Gill and a grunt escaped Sandi as she hungrily pulled herself up to find a mouth again.

"You animal!" She laughed after the kiss.

"You mind?" Sandi muttered, engrossed.

"I like being animals. It feels like being animals out here tonight, just us and the fields and sky."

"Exactly. It's how it should be. We're far too cooped up like rats in our cells." Which was all the conversation Sandi could manage as she worked her way down past Gill's waist with a private lick in the darkness across the skin of her stomach, until she could lift fabric away and lick more pressingly where she needed it. Gill slunk back on the seat and spread herself to receive the attention with a welcome sigh.

"Okay, I'm almost in no hurry to get back now." She just managed.

Sandi pulled back. "Isn't it just a beautiful thing though, outside at night?" And went back to work.

"My goodness, yes. Don't stop."

"Not plannin' to," came a muffled response.

But Gill found herself sliding off the bench and seeking her own treasure hunt.

"How I love this little denim skirt." Her hands felt their way along Sandi's hot skin and upwards on the outside of her thighs, tracing inwards waiting to hit fabric, but meeting only skin and her unashamed forest of hairs. Here she was so hot, and parting their way inwards her fingers were to be greeted by desire waiting and needing her.

"Oh, I should've known, all evening, that you'd have nothing much on."

"Now you know."

"Risky up on that stage, you know. Oh my," and with a final search for Sandi's mouth and a long, lingering kiss, she pulled herself away, "we *are* going to finish this at home...I'm practically in the mud..."

"Aww," came the faint protest.

"...for at least three reasons. A) I need a pee. B) I want to see you and lie on the comfort of my lovely bed with you and C) despite you being as hot as a bonfire on the fifth of November, and I mean that both as a compliment and literally, I'm still a bit chilly…"

Sandi pulled herself up until she had clasped Gill's hair, gently pinning it to her head and was breathing heavily in her ear.

Gill added, "But…I still want you to come hard, at home with me now. Come on."

She pulled herself up and leaned back, holding Sandi's hand, who had released her grip with her other hand.

"And…I don't want to rush…just because I'm cold. I want to linger."

"Oh my…" Sandi bent down to retrieve the bag. "We're jogging the last bit. Which could give me an interesting sensation, I can tell you," she said, achieving a laugh from them both and they set off at a faster pace to cover the remaining distance as quickly as was comfortable.

CHAPTER TWENTY

The quandary

In the middle of the night Sandi lay awake, Gill breathing evenly and steadily beside her, peacefully sleeping. The window was slightly ajar and she listened to the noises of the night, a rustle, the hoot of an owl. She imagined the party had beaten its way with the stomping of feet, clapping of hands and general high-spirited cheering into the early hours of the morning, but felt glad to be as if a thousand miles away from it in the quiet sanctuary of Gill's cottage. She could picture someone foolish like George Weaver having a funny turn and being sent home with an on the spot diagnosis of overheating and overdoing it, others wending their way homeward of their own accord with a warm buzz of camaraderie and goodwill spreading its communal cloak over the village. Not everyone had come. There were those who had no connection to the Heltons or Lisa's family and others who never liked going out for a gathering. No doubt there were a few who bore a grudge for some reason or showed only benign disinterest. She smiled to herself. There were always some in a village. The hall wouldn't have been large enough to cope with many more anyway.

She envisaged Inga calling for a taxi back to the Golf and Country Club where a pool and spa could make her trip feel a little more exotic, Mel hugging her on the pavement and making plans. Sandi closed that thought line down, just glad that Mel might be distracted away from her now. All hands would be put to the deck to clear away the hall once the band had finally packed up and were gasping a last beer at the bar. Tables would be carried away, chairs stacked, glasses collected and taken to the kitchen for washing in the morning, floors swept. Only a small twang of guilt crept through her at the thought. The others had excused her from these tasks gladly. Some of the relatives would have headed to small hotels, others were squeezed into the spare room or sofa at Lisa's family home, a few would have gone back to Helton Farm with John and Lisa. It might have made the traditionalists mutter that they should wait until the wedding, or that Lisa didn't qualify to wear white, but John was far down the road of being in charge of his own destiny, with only open-minded parents-in-law-to-be who had long-since given them their blessing to be a support for each other.

Still, it was their first 'official' night at Helton. Sandi knew it was happening. She knew they had sneaked nights when she was away. The signs of lipstick on a coffee mug or an accidentally left behind tooth brush were evidence enough in a house where the depth of the layer of dust on a surface was as familiar to her as her own face. She didn't mind at all, not remotely. Who was she to mind? She really liked Lisa; she loved John. She was all too familiar with the aching emotional void inside herself and John, or the instinctive desire that needed to be filled for John and Lisa. She wished everything for them that she hoped she had found too. It just left her with a little dilemma. Where did she fit in now?

CHAPTER TWENTY-ONE

Sacrifice at The Calf

The phone rang shrilly and abruptly. Sandi groaned, but Gill roused herself first, the call of an emergency ever-present on her mind. The phone's demands were her unwelcome companion. She smiled as she reached over Sandi, noticing the tangle of sheets and the asymmetrical fall of the duvet. They had fallen asleep, still entangled probably.

"Hell. Who's callin' at this time?" Sandi could be heard muttering, barely intelligibly.

But it was Sandi's mobile ringing, from her jacket, dropped onto the floor. Gill picked it up and answered. "Hello?"

Something was wrong. There was a tearful voice on the end, a gasping background noise, the sound of wind against the other phone and a crackle on the line. "Sandi?" The voice called out.

Gill nudged Sandi's shoulder. "Take it!" she whispered urgently, passing the handset over.

Sandi grasped the phone, shuffling herself onto the other elbow and prizing her eyelids apart. Gill checked the clock, ten fourteen, they had slept in, which was delightful, but this sounded bad.

Sandi was listening intently now and had swung legs off the bed, so that she now sat naked on the edge, her back to Gill. "Okay...calm down Mel. Have you called for help?" During the gaps at their end, the distraught crackle of a voice could be heard across the bed. "Good...that's good Mel...they'll be on their way...keep her still...and warm. Look...we'll be on our way. I can be there in about twenty minutes. Yes...I'll get her... I'm going now. I'll leave now. Bye. Calm down and breathe."

Sandi sat for a moment in stunned silence. Gill was already at her side waiting for information. Sandi squeezed her hand and simultaneously spoke, "That was Mel. They've been hiking, doing a sunrise walk or something daft, Inga's taken a fall at The Calf."

"Shit!"

"...near where we were talking about. Mel's called the emergency services. I suppose they'll send mountain rescue. But we should go—"

"Damn right...I'll go make coffee—"

"No time for that."

"A flask."

"Oh, yeah...sorry...and can you bring something medical... it's her ankle...she reckons, she can see the bone."

"Ugh! Sounds like an open, compound, maybe."

"We need to go. You okay to drive?"

"I wasn't that drunk!"

"Park at the Temperance and we'll walk it. That's quickest." They were already headed down the stairs and Sandi was diving into the bathroom, while Gill rushed around the kitchen gathering some supplies into a bag.

Within five minutes of the call they were in the car and on their way, still trying to shake the sleep from their heads.

"How long do you think it takes to scramble the mountain rescue team?" Gill wondered, as she reversed out of her parking space and turned to head up the mill track to the lane at the top.

"It depends. If they're sending the helicopter. That comes from Leeds, usually, or Thirsk. It took them about forty-five minutes when our folks crashed."

"Oh. I'm sorry. If it brings it all back."

"Don't worry yerself about that. I've been over that many a time in my head and with John. The what if…they'd been earlier? What if they hadn't swerved?"

Gill reached over and squeezed her thigh. Luckily, there had been a pair of Sandi's jeans still at Gill's house, drying from some previous muddy weekend excursion, so the unsuitable denim skirt had been left where it had been shed on the bedroom floor.

"I wonder how bad it is?" Sandi spoke again.

"Bad enough. If the bone's broken the skin, that's a hard fall. A nasty break, bleeding, which can add to the shock. It would need pinning, there'd be possible infection and we don't know how the rest of her is. I could hear groaning."

"Yeah, she was conscious."

"Well, that's a good sign, but painful for her."

"That would bloody well hurt. Next bend in the road, I might be able to see."

Neither of them spoke as they hurtled up the road and the car took the next corner, climbing above the tree line so that the valley below The Calf came into view, along with a distant glimpse of Kettle's Spout.

Sandi scanned the hillside. "Nothin'…pretty place to break your leg though."

"Small comfort. They were out walking really early."

"Yeah. Barely steady on their legs after last night I should think. Melonie ought to know better. We're nearly there. Pull in after the inn; there's road parking in the bays beside the bus stop."

It was true. The inn was only a few minutes' drive back up the road. They pulled in swiftly to the empty bays, jumped out and Gill shouldered the kit bag, locking up the car while Sandi scampered down the track over the rickety bridge. By the time Gill had crossed, Sandi was on top of the first hillock looking across to the cliffs beneath The Calf. She scrambled back down in billy-goat fashion, stumbling slightly in a pair of borrowed wellingtons.

"Careful, you'll turn your ankle too," Gill reprimanded her, but Sandi ignored this.

"Mel's practical enough about the hills. She'll be trying to be conspicuous."

"Call her."

"Yeah, of course." Sandi dug in a pocket for her phone. "God, this feels foreign. Phoning Mel. I've been trying to avoid having to do that for some time. But now's not the time to stand on principles."

Gill didn't bother responding, she was concentrating on trying not to pant out loud as she kept up with Sandi's buoyant pace on the springy turf.

"Here, let me take the pack." Sandi reached over for the bag, detaching it from one of Gill's shoulders, while she held her phone to her ear with the other. Gill gave up any attempt at fighting to maintain the dignity of being as fit as Sandi, letting her take the bag and swing it effortlessly onto her shoulder, while she still listened intently to the phone.

"Blast, no signal."

The rushing of the river, the picturesque hills, the blue clarity of the sky were only to be hurried by and briefly noted in passing.

"It's quite chilly," Gill gasped.

"And damp. Must've rained in the night. You could see why somebody would slip today."

Little rivulets of water trickled across the shale paths like miniature streams, as intent on their course as the river at the foot of the valley, purposefully returning to the sea. They were far enough around the headland of hills to be able to view the dark cliffs better now. They crossed a stone bridge and veered off the main path to take the often dangerous sheep track, the one that picked its way down from the top, the track that Gill had chosen to avoid on the day she had been angry with Mel, Sandi and herself.

"Seems the sirens claimed a victim today." Sandi chuckled with dark humor.

"Look!"

Suddenly, with the swerve of the path away from the valley floor and the steep climb already a hundred feet up, the figure of Mel could be seen, clad in a bright blue waterproof, hunched over the other crumpled figure, caught by a boulder several hundred feet further up and off the track by some distance.

"Blimey, she's on the edge of the crags."

"I wonder how far she fell?"

"I don't like the look of the scree between us and them."

Gill had felt for a whistle in her waterproof pocket. "Cover your ears."

Sandi caught on and obliged while Gill gave a shrill blast. Mel's distant figure stood and turned suddenly as the wind carried the noise to her. The figure started to wave frantically.

"Try calling again," Gill suggested.

Sandi pulled the phone from her pocket. This time was more successful. She was through and they watched the figure struggle to unearth its phone, before connecting to the familiar crackly, windy line of earlier.

"How's it going?"

Gill could hear Mel's high-pitched, anxiety-riddled reply through the receiver, on speaker. "Thank heavens! You're here. She's passed out. I'm so worried. I don't know what to do."

"Listen. I'll try to come across the scree. I'll put Gill on."

"Be careful." Gill and Mel chorused as Sandi handed the phone to Gill. She began edging her way onto it digging her feet in sideways to maximize the grip, attempting to create some sort of steps or path for herself. Gill, who hadn't continued the phone conversation yet, called out. "Perhaps we should wait for the rescue team, it doesn't look safe!"

Loose shale had started cascading down the hillside below Sandi's footsteps.

"You're not in the right gear!"

Sandi seem to have realized the same thing and had turned to retrace her steps briskly. The small stone avalanche she had created gamboled happily on down the hillside.

"Yep. Ah'm not doing that. Look at it. Nothing's stopping it. Let's go up the sheep track a bit further."

Gill nodded, slapping her on the back with some relief and lifted up. She needed to keep Mel calm, she realized. "Mel.

How on earth did you get down to her? It looks frighteningly unstable."

"I couldn't leave her like that. She'd fallen so awkwardly and the scream."

"Well, you've been unbelievably brave to get to her."

"Thanks."

"Tell me…if you put your hand to her neck…does she feel warm? Is she breathing okay?"

"Let me try."

She could see Mel at a distance, bending down, kneeling down.

"Yes, her skin's warmer than my hands there. She's breathing, but it's not normal…not relaxed…sort of shallow and fast."

"Is there much blood?"

There was a gulp. "I'll look, I covered it…" There was a pause, "…not masses, it's sort of slowed down."

"Okay. They're good signs. Sit down close with her and keep each other warm. Cover yourselves up with anything you have. Cover her injured leg gently again. Don't try to move her. Mel, eat a snack or have a drink. You need to be looked after too. We'll come up as high as we can safely. It's pretty slippery. But the rescue team can't be far. I'm going to get off the line now in case they're calling you. Watch us come up the hill. We're getting closer."

Gill ended the call and passed the phone up to Sandi. They needed to concentrate on their own ascent, which was becoming more treacherous. "Silly headstrong mare Inga."

"Hah!" Sandi laughed back at her, a few steps in front.

"Oops. Did I say that out loud?" Gill panted.

"Yep. You did. Are they good signs or are y' just being encouraging?"

"It depends…but I can't do much to help from here. This wasn't exactly how I wanted to start my lie-in with you."

"Me neither, but a friend in need…"

"…is a pain in the butt. Only joking. Actually feeling a tad guilty as we conspired to bring her over from Norway and pitch these two headstrong romantics together."

"Yeah." Sandi shouted back over her shoulder, "Why d'yer think I'm halfway up a mountain and not in bed with you this mornin'?" Even she was starting to gasp with the effort. They paused for a moment, catching their breath from the steep incline and looked back across the horseshoe-shaped valley. Kettle's Spout could be seen spilling down the opposite wall of the cliffs, the safer path just visible from time to time wending its way beside it and away again to negotiate the obstacles of the descent of that cliff.

"I'd rather be on that path. This one feels decidedly perilous."

"Let's get up to those rocks and wait. By the stunted tree."

"Good plan."

They continued up to where a cluster of rocks huddled against the hillside, providing some shelter from the continuous onslaught of the wind. No sooner had they set themselves down and hunted in the backpack for the flask, than the rhythmic thudding approach of the helicopter could be heard. At first it was just a distant drum beat, until suddenly it broke over the cliff above, becoming overpowering in its volume as the rotor noise echoed around the surrounding valley. It seemed to perform a couple of circuits, surveying the scene. Melonie was on her feet again, waving both arms madly in huge, grateful circles. Sandi and Gill sat tight, afraid of distracting them from their main target. Despite the desperate nature of the situation, it was a truly spectacular sight; like some giant, prehistoric, hunting insect, a massive, angry mosquito, drawn by the smell of blood and humans, and yet here full of hope and reassurance.

It performed one more loop and then came to rest, hovering above Mel and Inga. The other two girls watched as doors slid open and a silhouetted figure began to be winched down, the giant insect apparently unravelling itself or putting out some strange web. Conversation was impossible above the noise and the increased draught. The rescuer, presumably some sort of medic, touched down with precision accuracy along the rocks just a few paces away from their target, and at that distance, rapid assessments and the application of some sort of inflatable splinting system could only just be seen. Meanwhile the winch had gone up and was returning down again with a second member of the team, and some other equipment that appeared to be a stretcher. The figures remained in a huddle around Mel for some time, the minutes passing. Gill mimed the actions for an injection, drip and splint to Sandi, speculating on the treatment.

In no time at all, Inga was in the stretcher and one of the men steered her as they were winched up, the rescuer splaying himself and controlling the amount of spin in the wind. Once they were safely in, then the winch was returned to the ground to collect Mel and the other member of the rescue team. With a final wave from the helicopter, the rear doors were closed and the now apparently sated mosquito departed, leaving the hillside suddenly bare and silent save the surge of the wind and distant bleating sheep.

"That's that then. I suppose they'll go back to Leeds."

"Were we of any help at all I wonder?"

"I think Mel looked relieved to see us. It just so happened that the rescue team arrived soon after."

"Beautiful here isn't it?"

"A bit eerie, too."

"I know what you mean. Come on"—Gill pulled herself up to her feet—"I'm starving."

"And the inn does an excellent breakfast I hear."

"Last one down has to pay."

"Yes, okay, but no broken limbs please."

They paced carefully down the hillside, shale falling away from their footsteps, gravity working with them this time. Before long they were warming themselves gratefully in the large lounge of the Temperance Inn with a pot of coffee and two cooked breakfasts on the way. The landlord had been very communicative, indulging in enjoying the drama of the rescue story, which had been virtually on his doorstep.

"So that's a bonding experience for Mel and Inga." Sandi smiled wryly.

"You're a cruel woman! Not quite the one we had in mind."

"But still it'll do." Sandi grinned wickedly. "There'll be a good deal of hand patting and soul-searching going on."

"Really?" It was only an insincere admonition from Gill. "What I really want to chat to you about is…this arrangement up at Helton Farm. It doesn't seem right that you should feel uncomfortable in what is your house too."

Sandi poured out the coffee. "You're right there. I don't know if I'm coming or going at the moment."

"It's like you're being inched out, but politely! Although I don't think they mean it that way. It's just their lives finding the way forward. So what do you want to do about it? I mean, would you like to stay with me for a bit while you think things through?"

Sandi put down the coffee pot with a bump and stared hard at the lovely, thoughtful, honest woman opposite her. "Now there's an offer."

"Yes. And I meant it." Gill whispered. "But would you be able to get to milking on time or be there for an emergency in the night?"

"Well lambing's well and truly over and if I'm not there when he needs me then it only serves to emphasize that I'm missed." She paused to gather herself. "What has been playing at the back of me mind is using this stash of cash to convert the outlying barn that's barely used, the one on the edge of the field beyond the courtyard, it's almost a shell. But it's beautiful. High and airy, still with its old beams. That would make one hell of a home. There's enough cash from Mam and Dad to commission the architects in Blackford, keep it local, do it properly. That could make a great place."

"Stay with me while it's done."

"Move in with me when it's finished?"

"You're serious? What would John and Lisa say?"

"Yes, I'm perfectly serious. And I don't know what they'll say about my fledgling idea. But the farm needs me and John isn't going to mind a vet on the premises and us being happy, is he? And after all they're only borrowing half the farmhouse off me."

"What about Lisa? Is she open-minded enough to have us virtually on her doorstep?"

"Lisa? She's fine. She's a bit of a riot when you get a couple of glasses of wine down her. And potential babysitters on the doorstep? If I was that much of a pariah to the pair of them, it wouldn't have got this far."

"Pariah? Don't use that word. It's ridiculous. You're…" Gill hunted around for a suitable word and blushed as one spilled out, "…marvelous."

Sandi grinned massively at her and squeezed her thigh under the table. "And you're astonishing."

"Okay. Enough of the mutual admiration society. What about today? You're free aren't you?"

"I have all bloody weekend off my dear. If they're at the farm, they can have it for the weekend. John said as much, but the other way around, 'if we're here, you can have the weekend off pet'."

"Great. But I'm second on call at work."

"And if you have to go, I'll find something to do."

Their breakfasts arrived, distracting them from the conversation. Another family had planted themselves noisily at a nearby table, clattering the cups and arguing over the menu.

"Did I tell you I swam with dolphins once?" Sandi threw in as an aside.

"You did mention it. Tell me again. How? Where?"

"I was driving back along the coast road to go back to college in Wales, you know, looking out at sea from time to time and daydreaming, when I saw them. A pod of dolphins jumping and flipping, not far out. There wasn't a soul around, so I pulled up on the next parking lay-by and stripped off and dived in."

"I love this story."

"Yep. They were curious, once I swam out they came around and nosed at me, investigating me, like I was some alien in their world. Which I suppose I was. They were gentle and very smooth."

"I would have liked to have seen that. And joined in come to think of it. Can I come too next time?"

"There you go again. Setting me off with a phrase like that. We'll have to pay up and go back to our lie-in."

"What about Inga?"

"We can't do more than the hospital is doing can we? Mel's bound to call later when she has news. There'll be a lot of waiting for them to do."

"X-rays and so on. Probably an operation from the sounds of that fracture. But we must go later."

"I know. We will. The best thing we can do, I mean overall for the future outcome, is leave them to sort it out for now... come on."

CHAPTER TWENTY-TWO

When the path crumbles.

Chatting happily, Gill, driving, sneezed massively. They were on their way to meet Andrew and Becka, some weeks later. Enough time had passed that Inga had healed sufficiently well, nursed attentively by Mel, for the two of them to return to Norway. Hospital and home visits had been made, bridges mended and Mel was eager to help the patient on her journey home. A general sense of relaxation had descended.

Sandi doubled up with laughter. The sneeze had come from nowhere, hilariously noisy, brought on by hay cutting perhaps, arriving suddenly. Like the lorry that came from somewhere, Manchester probably, swinging too far out around the bend to clear the stonewall with its load, brought on by haste trying to reach its pick-up in Wensleydale or similar. There was barely a millisecond to think. Gill instinctively swerved left to avoid a head-on collision. Sandi had started a scream, a thousand memories bursting in on her instantaneously, the millisecond slowing to an eternity.

Their car careered through the fence on the left, only clipping the marked pillars that warned of the dangerous bend. Over the low wall, its under-chassis catching there, it hung there, for what must have been five seconds, deciding which way its load would take it, balanced precariously, teetering first forward, then back, then finally deciding forward was what it was most used to it tipped, nose down, which was just enough momentum to take the front end over the wall, touch the front wheels down, which turned with the movement, upending the rear sufficiently to take the weight over the wall, the back wheels simply aiding the direction as they followed over the ancient bricks.

Not a mark on it at that point, it appeared to look at the precipitous incline, the land dropping away towards the steep valley, deciding it would like the journey, it headed off down the field, and subsequently on down the hill, gaining momentum rapidly, until clipping an outcrop of rock it tipped sideways, beginning the sideways roll that accelerated and sent it plunging, momentum ever-increasing out of sight.

The lorry driver had not seen this, aware perhaps that a car had come suddenly around the corner, had maybe swerved a little to avoid him, but the container on the rear and his eye to the clock had blocked any further concerns. The vehicle had headed on normally to take the next major road through the valleys. The short cut had been of use to the schedule.

Eventually the car came to rest at the line of trees, some way down the incline. It lay on one side, the bodywork now disfigured.

* * *

Andrew and Becka waited happily at the pub, presuming only a slight delay for traffic, a phone call, some other pit stop or a last minute urgent snog.

* * *

At the fleeting moment of seeing the lorry appear, all that Sandi had visualized about her parents' accident stormed in on her. She had shrieked, but the rising noise caught in her throat and was stopped by some inner valve. Visions and thoughts crowded in at the speed of light.

Gill had turned the wheel left, apparently instinctively. Not because it was necessarily a safer choice overall, but just avoiding the immediacy of the impact. Sandi had seen in that split second that her instinct would have been to do the same. She felt herself ricochet at the moment of impact as the car hit the wall. Stunned, she was aware of the pause in their momentum.

"Get out!" She heard herself yelling, as if disembodied, with the intensity that only an emergency could bring. "Get the fuck out!" Like a reflex, she released both the seatbelt clasps and was shoving Gill forcibly, fiercely by the shoulder, toward the door.

Gill turned to look at her, trancelike. Her face was unrecognizable with fear. Sandi snarled angrily, trying to break through to the startled wide eyes, feeling a drip of blood on her face. "NOW!" she screeched wildly. She had kicked her own door open wide and reached over to punch Gill's door open, hurting her knuckles in the process. One more punch at Gill's shoulder and she was out. Gone. Sandi went to step out of her own door, the alighting leg met only air, and she fell out a few feet onto the ground, winding herself, lying on the turf gasping like a fish out of water. Recovering, she watched as the car tipped forward, plummeting down the hill.

For a brief moment, their fates had headed toward joining the spirits on the moors, perhaps to become a pair of ghostly frolicking water nymphs in some remote pool, to be seen only by an occasional passerby.

Sandi struggled over to Gill, grasping her tightly. She could feel her trembling, perhaps in shock. It seemed to rouse Gill to some semblance of reality and she started checking herself over for signs of damage. She pulled herself up into a sitting position, disentangling Sandi's arms with some difficulty as they had locked themselves around her shoulders.

Sandi hugged her knees and started rocking gently forward and backward, not quite in the land of the living. A thin trickle of blood had drizzled its way from her hairline down her left cheek. Evidently alarmed, Gill turned her attention to finding the wound.

"Don't worry, just a small cut, no sign of heavy trauma, raised or indented." She was murmuring on autopilot. "Still, concussions are to be taken seriously. I'm so sorry." She was whispering, "I will never drive again."

Sandi was silent, until she managed, "Don't be silly, you daft cow…it was that idiot lorry swinging out."

"I don't know."

"Sure as hell was. You didn't get his number plate?"

"No way…too fast."

"That's what I thought too."

She had stopped rocking herself.

"You all right?" Gill urged gently.

"No, ah bloody well am not. My life and my parents' lives have just all flown in front of my eyes."

"Jeez…I'm so sorry."

"Will you stop it."

"Sorry."

"Stop."

"Okay." They stared at each other.

"We're in one piece anyway," Sandi tried.

"Only just." Gill levered herself up into a more comfortable position, dug in a pocket and found a tissue to dab at Sandi's head. "See…"

"Oh…owwch. I hadn't noticed. Not so sure about the car either."

It lay on its side. It didn't look like it was going anywhere for a while. Some sheep had started drifting toward it, nosing curiously at the strange creature that had arrived unexpectedly in their field.

"You stay put. I'm going to take a look and fetch what I can." Gill started to lever herself up, looking shaky.

"Yes. Whatever you say doctor. But you don't look too great yourself."

"Shut up."

Sandi pushed herself onto her feet and tried herself out. Her right ankle felt jarred and her neck had a strange, slightly jelly-like, disembodied feel, but everything seemed to move. She lowered herself cautiously to the ground as Gill limped down the field, looking thoroughly peeved. The sheep observed her too with some interest, those that didn't scatter at her approach holding their ground to watch the spectacle.

A sense of peace descended, and Sandi recognized shock as she waited, as if time had stood still.

After a while, filled only with the call of crows and the occasional 'bah' of sheep, Gill reappeared, panting and limping slightly, weighed down with what she could carry up the hill. She dropped bags and coats to the floor, bending over, hands on her knees, recovering her breath. "One of the doors has come off the car," she gasped initially and catching her breath added, "there are dents in the bodywork. Everything has been shaken up and spread randomly inside, a loose bandage from the opened glove compartment has draped itself like a party banner across the headrests." She gasped and dropped to the turf. "My handbag had exploded, which meant I had to rummage around, tentatively climb in, to search for my wallet, phone and so on. Luckily that bag hadn't opened." She nodded at her workbag, with its industrial-strength clasps. This speech seemed to finish her off and she fell back on the grass, splayed out with the effort.

"Give me a minute and I'll see to your cut." She added feebly.

They both lay there, stunned for a moment, until Gill hauled herself back up to sitting to clean and stick Sandi's cut, which she tolerated with barely a whine. Then Sandi got to her feet, checking herself for dizziness on Gill's advice, but finding none they both made a return trip, Sandi checking the car to make sure it wasn't about to burst into flames and afterward bringing their belongings to the top of the hill just below the broken wall. By this point another car had slowed down, pulling up to a standstill on realizing the circumstances. Sandi was on her phone, through to Andy and Becka, who were on their way.

The kindhearted passersby pulled out a flask of reviving coffee, insisting upon calling the police, although unfortunately they themselves could be of little more assistance not having any knowledge of the offending lorry from their journey further down the road. They left a number to call, in case they could be of any other help, the driver checked their vehicle briefly and they departed, leaving the two of them to wait cuddled together inside their jackets.

"I've gone off the idea of the campervan," Sandi murmured.

"Yep. For now."

"I've gone off the idea of going out for the evening."

"Uh-huh. I just want to get home."

"Me, too."

"Hot baths and maybe a curry later?"

"Just home to Helton." She was shuddering again. Trying to make light of it, she added, "Er...what happens with the car?"

"The police can get it towed. Or the insurance...I'm not sure."

Andy and Becka arrived, distressed for them, bundling them and everything they could find around them or in the crashed car into theirs.

"What about the police?" Gill asked.

"I've left them a note on the car," Becka replied.

"We can't just leave the scene." Gill worried.

"It says so on the note."

"You're starting to shake again." Gill commented.

"You try holding *your* hand out then." Sandi snapped slightly.

Gill obliged. Her fingers were trembling.

"I'm no superhero." She admitted.

Andy maneuvered the car, heading back to Blackford.

"Bloody hell fire," Sandi added.

"Yeah. It nearly was."

Strangely, they found themselves laughing.

CHAPTER TWENTY-THREE

The paths diverge

The phone rang insistently, with an attitude that struck Gill as particularly urgent. Urgency appeared to be the theme of the day: a caesarean section on a cow, a cat hit by a car, a fox with a broken leg at the animal sanctuary. She hauled herself away from her perch in the back garden overlooking the roaring river, bringing her barely touched glass of wine with her. What would it be now she wondered?

The display flashed up Helton Farm's number. She smiled; maybe Sandi had plans for her at last. Things had gone strangely dead between them since the car accident. She knew what it was—the accident had been a shock, bringing back memories. Having the police call, raking over the incident, a statement required from the insurance company, the added bonus of whiplash thrown in. It had dug it all up again, adding to the burden Gill felt for being the driver. She'd left messages for her, caught her briefly for a quick word at the supermarket, but it had seemed best to let her simmer for a while. And did it not occur to her that Gill was feeling crap about it too? How could she think it was only about herself?

But it was not Sandi's mellow voice that greeted her. Instead it was John sounding worried on the other end. Was Sandi with her? She hadn't been seen since last night. He'd presumed they'd had a spontaneous moment, but she hadn't returned to oversee the first hay cut on the lower meadow as planned. He was anxious, she hadn't been completely herself since the road accident, inclined to make off-the-cuff moody remarks or distractedly stare out into the distance. Gill agreed. They hadn't seen quite so much of each other for a week or two. She had thought she was just preoccupied with the farm and was miffed with her for the crash.

"Gosh, no!" John exclaimed. "Not you! She thought you'd saved your lives. But I think it's stirred everything up again about, y'know, Mam and Dad. Gill, I'm a bit concerned. To be honest I don't think she's dealt with it all, I mean, y'never do completely do you? But it hit us hard back then. She's never had a holiday. Ever. It's wrong. I should have pushed her to take a break."

"What never?"

"Exactly. She's bogged off for a few weekends here and there. But, look, I'm just afraid she's gonna crack up. Will you have a go at finding her?"

"I'm right on it."

"I'm goin' down to the village to ask around if she's been seen lately."

"Call me if you get news, on the mobile."

"Right-ho."

Gill hung up, put the entire glass of white wine into the fridge, in the hope it would be finished in company later and set to packing a small backpack with a few bits, snacks and medical supplies, again, just in case. But she didn't feel very disturbed. Sandi was a rock, as solid and permanent-feeling as the land itself, and she could feel her heart beat still contentedly part of her own. She was convinced she would know if something was really wrong with her.

She grabbed a quick bite of a slice of bread, shoved her waterproof, boots and bag into the back of her new car, a replacement for the written-off wreck, and locked the cottage. Charlie fretted around her feet, marked his scent at the Daily Post, his usual fence pole, then hopped into the car. The hills glowered at her, like Sandi in one of her dour moments. If she was anywhere it would be in one of her hideaways, somewhere out there, far from the madding crowd, feeling the pulse of the earth for reassurance.

John's plan was good. Someone in the village could well have seen her. She drove in, parking up in the central car park next to the Tourist Information Office and started making enquiries. But the trail was cold.

Feeling the weariness of the day creeping upon her, she was racking her brains about what to do next, when she saw John coming out of the bakery. The shop was almost closed. The shutters were already down. He was on his mobile and hers had just started to ring in her pocket, so she scampered across to catch him in person.

"Hi!" She greeted him with a kiss on the cheek, as had become their habit. "News?"

"Yep, she bought a few provisions from the bakery early this morning, enough for a small picnic. Dressed to walk, boots, bag et cetera."

"Oh, that's good then. Sounds organized."

"Yeah, silly mare, worrying me like that. Not answering her phone."

"Anything more?"

"Not a lot. But Rita, y'know, behind the counter, asked her where she was off to and she said she was taking to the hills."

"Okay, that gives me a pretty good idea. No need to call the emergency services just yet." She half-joked. "You head back up to the farm if that's fine with you, to let me know if there's news from there, I'm going to try The Calf. There's something about that place this summer. It's where *I* went when I was in a mood once and this is where I'd buy myself a pie if that's where I was going."

"But it's a bit late in the day to start that. And her four by four's at home."

"Yeah, that's a bit odd, I must admit. But it's the best plan I have and it won't be dark for five hours."

"Well, keep in touch with me then."

"Absolutely." They hugged. "I'll try not to worry."

"If you need something else to think about, start looking at the farm diary and booking us in a holiday!"

"It wasn't me who prevented it from happenin'. It was her!"

"Yeah, I know, stubborn mare."

They laughed awkwardly.

* * *

Gill had climbed steadily, deep in thought. Not a little disturbed by the knowledge of Sandi's more temperamental, impetuous moments. It was like living with the changeable weather. She smiled to herself. Well, they were all used to living with that. By the time she had achieved the second rise after Winder, she could see along the ridge top.

And there she was…Sandi at the top of The Calf, deep in thought.

She must have known the rhythm and weight of Gill's approaching step, because she was murmuring as Gill approached close enough to hear:

"I see her or hear her…the spirit…she was like me."

This was a disconcerting start.

"No she wasn't," Gill began uncertainly.

"The story said her father hated her."

"Yours didn't."

"I lied."

Gill needed a moment to digest this fact. "Why would you do that?"

"The truth is harder to face."

"What…your father hated you?"

"Well, perhaps hate is too strong…" she paused. "He just didn't *get* me, didn't understand. Why could I be that perverted not to like the several suitable young lads in the village?"

"*Perverted*? Are you sure you're not reading more into this after the fact. I mean"—she trod carefully—"I've met John. He's absolutely right on the mark with it all."

"Yeah…younger generation. Mam said Pa would come around eventually…but I never had time to find out, because of…"

"Oh…but still, isn't this the fable of the maiden at The Calf the *other* way around?"

"How d'ya mean?"

"He's gone…it's tragic…but if there were any shackles, they're off now. She, the maiden, had no way to remove the shackles. So the story goes, she jumped or fell. You're not planning on that?"

Sandi managed a wry smile. "Is that what you were thinking?"

"Maybe…when I saw you here after nobody knew where you'd been for the past twenty-four hours."

"Only twelve hours, I just got up early and left."

"And didn't tell a soul."

"Do I *have* to tell someone my every movement?" she snapped slightly.

"No. Of course not. But John was wondering. I care about you, that's all that matters about this now."

"I cared about him."

Gill had a sudden realization she had said something wrong.

"I dunno. I just can't get my head around it. I can't shake his disapproval off. I'm not sure I can do this now. It's too much."

"Do *what*?"

"Be with you, make a commitment."

"Well, that's come a bit out of the blue. *You've* been driving it forward."

"Y'think?" She was aggressive, then sheepish. "Yeah, I know." A flash of something darker crossed her eyes. "But I need you to go now…I need to think."

Gill's patience cracked. "Well, fuck it. I'm not leaving you up here to lick your wounds whatever you think about *us*. You think I need to be messed about? I'm the stranger in this place.

You bloody well start walking back down the Winder Path and I'll watch you from a distance. I'm not walking with you in this mood." She paused, confused, adding quietly, "But we want you to be safe."

"That's nice." A trace of sarcasm flickered across Sandi's face. "I'm not walking with you either." It sounded petulant and with it she stood up, shouldered her pack, turned her back and strode off, back the way from which Gill had arrived.

The sun was starting to set and the view back across the fells was stunning, breathtaking, the sky streaked with orange. But Gill's heart had started to leak and as she watched the tall, loping figure depart, far enough away for a respectable distance between them. She followed more slowly, a burning pain beginning in her throat and head. She pressed hard into her temples as tears started and stung her eyes.

When the opportunity arose to take a side path down towards the Leeson Farm, she took it, turning her back on Sandi.

After all, it was exactly what Sandi had done to her. Confused, she increased her speed and stumbled down the slope as quickly as she could to return to her own bolt-hole and slam the door shut on an episode she wanted desperately to compartmentalize away.

Her glass of wine in the fridge looked forlorn now. Momentarily representing loneliness. Having shrugged off her bag, but keeping her coat on, she took the glass back out into the garden.

Her former peaceful reverie had gone from her. The sun was lower in the sky, the air cooler. She leaned over the back fence, looking into the gorge. A dipper was darting across the rocks higher up in the stream. She felt exhausted. It had been a hell of a day. Her feet were aching from the sudden effort of the hike.

The stinging in her eyes and throat had died down as she descended from the hill, to be replaced by a bitter taste in her mouth and some rising anger. She had sent a brief message to John: *Found her. On her way home. In a foul mood with me. Don't know why.*

She was too tired. A little numb from the unexpected outburst. Wrong-footed. Suddenly not knowing this person. She almost felt too tired to care.

Let her be a complete madam, she thought.

How could someone have such a lack of self-awareness? Such a fine border between self-centeredness and self-awareness. The former being self-absorbed. The latter being helpfully self-critical with a view to the effect it might have on *other* people. Perhaps Sandi was one of those people who failed to see the effect their behavior had on those around them. The 'devil-may-care' attitude spilling over into callousness about other people's feelings. The 'if you choose to react in that way that's not my fault' attitude.

Was Sandi more screwed up than Gill had ever realized?

She suddenly felt even wearier. She couldn't be bothered to feel any emotion and realizing that, sat quietly back down onto the garden bench, sipping her wine, watching for bats along the river as the sun went down on a day full of too much drama.

* * *

Sandi had not turned to look back until she descended the Winder Path, the village now closer in view. It was only then that she noticed Gill had gone. Fuming with a hundred petty slights, hypothetical errors and descending into a fuming turmoil of her own, she had been stomping along, furious at being herded, picturing Gill sulking along behind her.

Expecting to be able to turn and glare at Gill with some strange satisfaction, her absence suddenly burst the self-inflated bubble of her own anger.

Gone. She was gone.

Sandi stopped abruptly, her lungs working hard. Where she had been muttering *stupid cow* to herself, now she could think of nothing. She stood blinking in the setting sun like a winded bullock, beginning to feel idiotic. She scoured the hills behind her with her eyes, but in the fading light and long shadows there was no movement apart from a few birds.

Looking down at the village, she shook her head.

Gone.

Was that really what she wanted?

She started to run heavily down the hillside, feeling her knees, thighs and calf muscles pound with the effort. Her eyes prickled. With the effort, she thought. Stupid cow. She echoed and she no longer felt as convinced that it was directed at Gill.

What a fuck up.

It was more of a hint of an acknowledgement than the blacksmith's hammer blow it deserved. She reached the steps carved into the lower section of the path by the National Trust and slowed to a more civilized pace to enter the village without attracting unnecessary attention.

Once past the bakery and supermarket, she went up a gear and hurried on her homeward journey. What *did* she want? She hadn't been forced into a corner like this for some time and felt her wilder instincts at war with themselves.

Change. It was time for a change, but it was like it was being forced upon her. She was rubbish at change. She knew it and tried to avoid it. In the past it had brought too much…*pain.* But what was this if it wasn't pain? It bloody well hurt her head and her heart. And something deeper.

She pushed on to the farm as hard as she could, climbing the opposite hillside at a fast pace in the fading light, the physical activity forcing thoughts away. John would have something to say to her. She knew he would. She started to have an awareness that maybe she deserved it, but inside, she was just in turmoil.

CHAPTER TWENTY-FOUR

Alone

Weeks went past. Gill immersed herself in work, a busy time of year for farrowing and calving. When she had any spare time, she socialized with her colleagues. If they noticed her increased availability, they kept their own counsel.

Her one weekend off during this period, she headed to the city on the Saturday for the first time since she had been in Yorkshire.

Still shaken from the accident, she chose to go to Manchester for the day by train just to relax, which took longer than she had planned, but still enabled time for lunch in Harvey Nichol's café and an afternoon of spoiling herself, splashing out on some new clothes, taking a massage at the Beauty Parlor . It was refreshing to leave the farm smells behind, not being the rustic cousin for a change.

Sunday, she drove south to Malham Cove and took Charlie on a hard walk past Janet's Foss waterfall, a peaceful lagoon, and up through the harsh, rocky climb of Gordale Scar to the limestone pavements at the top, carrying Charlie at times where the cliffs were toughest. Looking out over the two hundred and fifty meter drop, where the peregrine falcons circled, she wondered to herself. Was she missing Sandi? Yes of course, particularly as she hiked through such a stunning place, where she could imagine her frolicking in the water or setting a strenuous pace. But it was good to be left to her own thoughts and her own pace too, and she wouldn't let it eat away at her and ruin everything. It was her own stupid fault, she told herself, for mixing business with pleasure, and it had all become just a little bit too much of a roller coaster recently.

She had been self-sufficient before. She could be so again. She swallowed down the dart of emotional pain that stung her somewhere inside.

When she arrived back in the village, back at Blackford, she found herself at a loose end so went to browse the enormous stock of secondhand books again in the Old Library building. The musty, dusty smelling environment was endearingly comforting. In the local section she had pulled a pile of likely books off the shelves, following Bridget's advice to read up about her community's history. *Blackford—Historical Accounts* dealt with history recent enough to have old black and white photos of devastating floods, fallen trees or tipped lorries, with some unlikely stories of ghosts in the attics or fallen soldiers who had come home in spirit. Gill's skin stood to attention as she read the supernatural stories. She found herself unable to resist hunting for the *Local Myths and Legends* booklet and discovered it still sandwiched where she had hidden it. She read the Winder legend again, less chilled by it now it was so familiar, then flicked through the rest of the booklet. A couple of appendices on names caught her eye and sure enough, running her finger down the columns, she came across 'Helton' meaning 'from the hillslope' adding 'an old, hardy Dales name.'

She smiled to herself, pleased with the definition that confirmed her opinion. She had started to see Sandi so much more clearly, a free spirit, connected to her environment, but damaged, injured like a wounded bird needing to regrow some lost primary feathers and regain confidence. Meanwhile, the damage left her vulnerable and defensive, quick to bite back or withdraw when she felt too exposed. Always needing the freedom to fly.

This time she felt assured enough to buy the booklet. She would tuck it, hide it, in one of her bookshelves.

CHAPTER TWENTY-FIVE

Guidance

Plans for the barn conversion were going at full drive. John had pushed for action on all fronts. He had motivated a slightly listless Sandi to formulate her ideas, the architects to put everything down, the bank to move the funds, the builders to get cracking. He was not in the least little bit prepared to allow his life to be tidy with Lisa, his life to flourish, without seeing his sister's life have the same potential.

Although, it appeared there was some sort of barrier to that happening. He had finally become aware, in the way that only the closest of relatives or friends can be, that his apparently resilient sister was perhaps closer to breaking point than he had realized.

He had sat her down one evening after a tough day on the farm, determined to plumb the hazardous emotional depths.

They had discussed the day, the building works, the next few weeks of farm work. A whisky down, as was their way, and he had broached the subject with characteristic brevity.

"So what's up, Sis?"

"Er…whad'ya mean?"

"Doh!" He impersonated Homer Simpson, striking his forehead with the flat of his hand. "Haven't seen any cute vets round here lately."

"No flies on you." Sandi paused. "I don't want to talk about it."

"Oh really? Well I won't top your whisky up until you do."

Sandi twisted her tumbler thoughtfully.

"Fucked up, didn't I?"

John let the words hang in the air. Waiting.

"And there's the barn taking shape. And I'll be rattling around in it by myself."

"Why?"

"That's the question. Why? That's what I've tried to ask myself. And I can't bloody well answer it." She paused for thought. "The closest I've got is that I don't think I can do change. Makes me panic," she added grudgingly at the end.

John stared into his glass. "Mum and Dad isn't it?"

"Dunno, maybe." She resorted to childlike sulkiness.

"That was a *terrible* change. Maybe some change can be good. Beneficial."

"Yeah, I don't doubt it. It's just…things are changing fast again and it's risky…I can't tell if it will be…good."

"Look—"

"Don't preach."

"Do I ever?" He grinned. "It's like Bob's dog."

"*What?*"

"Y'know, Bob Kent's dog. Hit by a car and survived."

"You're not comparing me to a dog?"

"Yeah…course."

He caught her eye and grinned again. Suddenly she was laughing.

"Yeah…Bob's dog." He continued. "Bob's dog, clipped by a car unexpectedly and quite badly, when he was happily chasing a ball. Life was good, suddenly it wasn't. An animal doesn't know why it is suddenly in pain, being messed about at the vet's, feeling shit for a week or so."

"And this is me?"

"Wait for it…Bob's dog now hates cars, no…not hates…is terrified of cars and walks. An agoraphobic dog. Any car noise and walk…the world is out to get him. Tail between his legs at the first sound or sight. He doesn't know where from or if the pain will come again, unexpectedly. So Bob sent him to therapy."

Sandi guffawed loudly. "*Therapy?*"

"Bridget sent him to York. Bob's dog on his holidays in York. For a week. Covered by insurance apparently. Can you imagine it? Suitcase in paw. Handkerchief knotted on his head. Passport, ticket, money…bones."

Sandi had relaxed. John pressed on, aware he was winning.

"So what happened?" Sandi's curiosity was piqued, he could tell.

"Therapy sessions? Aqua aerobics for canines. I dunno. Gentle dog training and tranquillizing. Like 'this is a *car*…but if you stay on the lead with your owner on the pavement you get a treat and life's okay?' Anyway, it worked, fairly well. He's not bad. As long as Bob walks him with a load of treats in his pocket and a lead handy, the dog's okay. Meek as a newborn lamb when it comes to going back on the lead. Bob's dog. Life is good-ish again. But maybe never quite the same as it was before."

"The moral to the story being?"

"Mum and Dad. It shook us both up. Unexpectedly and painfully. We're burnt by that experience. So we know it— life—can hurt, unexpectedly. Once bitten, twice shy, as they say. So it might hurt again. Perhaps life can only ever be good-ish for us. Perhaps we'll always be a little bit like Bob's dog. But what if that, Mum and Dad going, was one of the worst possible shocks that can happen? We've carried on, and made a pretty good fist of it, how much time has passed? How many times has life delivered a blow as bad as that *again?* We were doing pretty well. Until along came your close shave with the car…and Gill driving. Like it can happen *again* and with someone you *love?* With *her?* It's too risky. Life is too risky. It might hurt *that much again*, y'know…like Mum and Dad…or *worse?*"

Sandi was just staring at him, open-mouthed.

John didn't bat an eyelid. He reached across and poured some more whisky into her glass.

"It's never stopped us before. You *have* to carry on, fight the fight, make some choices, go with a gut feeling. We wouldn't have this great shorthorn herd if we had let the 'what-ifs' stop us from getting it started."

"That's life."

"Exactly…that's bleedin' life, that is. You go with a gut feeling, the one that feels right at the time, something good comes of it, sometimes shit happens as they say. It's all part of life. Hay in one end—nice and tasty—shit out the other, I'll spare you the description."

Sandi roared with laughter at him.

Once she had calmed herself enough, she practically shouted at him. "You're a bloody genius, you are."

She took a long sip of whisky and speaking more quietly added, "You're going to make a great dad."

He laughed. "Not just yet, give me a few years of making hay while the sun shines first. Before the shit happens, y'know… baby shit." He grinned at her. "You'll be a great babysitter."

"You wish."

"Yeah, and a great girlfriend, if you'd just let yourself be."

"I wonder how she's doing?"

"Bit peeved, I should think."

"You've seen her!"

"Just phone messages." He paused. "She doesn't know what she's done. She doesn't know the why either."

The conversation hung in the air.

"Thanks." She stood up and went over to him, bending down to give him a hug and a peck on the cheek. "Love ya!"

"Love ya, too."

"I'm going to check the barns then hit the sack. Thanks again," she added as she left the room.

"You're welcome. Add it to the tally of babysitting nights you owe me."

"You wish." She called again. "Actually I won't mind." She grinned at him and threw him a surrendering wave as she headed out into the yard.

CHAPTER TWENTY-SIX

The dream

Gill was walking in a wood. Quite a dense wood. It was strangely dark, an odd time to be taking a walk, she thought vaguely to herself, and the atmosphere was unusually misty. It was peculiarly difficult to think too. As if her legs and brain were not quite connected. Her favorite analytical tool, her brain, seemed to be working okay, just distractedly.

*Oh, this is a dream...*she realized, as she stepped around another tree. The bark was rough, like a pine, moist too and with dark, healthy-looking moss growing on one side of it. The trees were growing closely together. A man-made forest, the trees disturbingly close together, on the claustrophobic side. Making it slightly harder to breathe, with no fresh breeze. The air felt fetid.

A noise startled her. She turned abruptly to look, although her feet would not move quickly. A small Muntjack deer was bolting into the forest gloom. Aware of everything, she searched around again, beginning to feel a weird mixture of unnaturally calm and slightly afraid. Cold too. On the path in front of her was a hind leg of a deer. Just that. Only the leg, taken at the ball joint. Unpleasant. She shuddered. Perhaps the wood housed a fiercer animal than the deer. Something predatory. She moved forward, unable to prevent herself, or to wake up, a thought that crossed her mind briefly somewhere in the deep layers.

A brighter, hazy light drifted between the trees ahead. Perhaps a spot of sun in a clearing. She followed it, intending to find space or a way out.

But the clearing did not appear.

Abruptly, the light appeared in front of her. Sidling out from behind a larger tree. It was vaguely human-shaped. Paranoia hit her in a tidal wave. A panic so huge it was blinding to all her senses. *Run!* But she could not move. All nerve endings refusing.

The shape reached out and took her by the wrist with its bright hazy light. Suddenly they, she and *it*, were standing on the edge of a precipitous cliff, at the foot of which crashed the sea in abominable, stormy waves far below in the twilight.

The thing spoke into her thoughts, no words seeming to present themselves. *Choose.* Danger was imminent. That's all Gill's startled senses could feel. Adrenaline. She could not choose, could not do anything.

She stood there frozen by the presence of the light form, blank in her mind. Until suddenly, her ability to choose forced its way through the panic and murkiness: *I choose to wake up!*

She sat up in bed. Her hair fell clumsily around her face.

"Ugh!" Her heart was still thumping. *Or you lose.* The thing released its grip, but the words echoed in her subconscious.

Pushing herself upright, she reached for the side light, her skin covered in goose bumps, her mouth dry. Charlie sat up on the bed and made a low whine in his throat. She put her hand distractedly onto his comforting, warm flank. The low light sent long shadows all over the room. She glugged down the glass of water next to her bed, stood up unsteadily and looked over the balcony railing. Charlie jumped off the bed to follow her, hanging questioningly around her heels. An uncharacteristic sense of vertigo lingered from the dream. She pulled on a wrap, went to the rear window and looked out towards the dark line of the hills, vaguely outlined in the night sky and the faintest of morning light beginning in the eastern ridge.

Choose or you lose.

She knew she would not be able to sleep for the remainder of the night, even though part of her was dog-tired. Her heart was still thudding. *What was that?* She questioned herself as she descended the stairs, cautiously on slightly wobbly legs. *A haunting?* Charlie scampered past her, his claws tapping on the wooden stairs, due for a nail clipping.

Don't be so stupid.

It was her subconscious working out her problems. That was what all dreams were. Brain activity. The scientific side of her tried to force its way back to reality. But what did it mean?

She put on the coffee machine and threw the back door open. A chill stream of air rushed around her bare ankles. Charlie went out for a call of nature. The anxiety began to subside.

Then she noticed that for the first time in weeks, she had not woken up feeling depressed about Sandi. It had been the first feeling that surged into her empty body each morning or night call that had woken her since their bitter exchange.

She felt…*clean* again. Choose or you lose? Is that what the dream wanted to tell her?

Four forty-five in the morning. *Ugh!* But sometimes it was better to be up than asleep. A creepy feeling hovered over her. She suppressed the thought that the little booklet hidden in her library of books was throbbing at her, mockingly. She made the coffee, closed the back door once the dog was in and took the mug to curl up in her comfortable armchair. She pulled a veterinary magazine onto her lap, opened it and stared at it blankly. Charlie settled into his basket, licking the dew off his paws and paused to watch her from time to time.

Choose Sandi? Choose to ignore Sandi? She could hardly choose her if it was no longer an option. Her thoughts whirled unhelpfully.

Choice and timing…it was so easy to get it wrong. The wrong time might mean catching someone else at a bad moment. Not speaking up, that could mean losing a chance forever. Decisions about work had been easier to make. But people? She didn't feel any further forward in her mind. She could flee? Leave Yorkshire? Start again somewhere else.

That idea felt fundamentally wrong. She hadn't been here long. It would look suspicious on the next job application. And Sandi…had they really given up, or was it just a hiatus, or a blip? Leaving Yorkshire was a last resort. She liked it here. The job was fulfilling, the people had been mostly friendly and supportive. She was starting to understand that she was a country dweller too. The space…room to breathe.

Choose or you lose.

Her left wrist burned with an icy cold feeling, where the ghostly figure had grasped her.

CHAPTER TWENTY-SEVEN

Convergence

Sandi booked an appointment at the vet's surgery. The online appointment page read: *Farm cat annual jabs*. Becka, who had been spectacular in collusion on receiving the call and hearing her enfeebled explanation, signed her into the computer system as John H. to be altered after the event.

So when Gill had called. "Next..." while wiping down the examination table, she did not at first see who came into the room, closing the door behind them.

"Hi," Sandi volunteered flatly. "How are you?"

Gill spun around, the cloth dangling from her hand.

"Sandi!"

"Yep, that's my name. But I wouldn't be surprised if you weren't exactly delighted to hear it."

"Well..."

"Here's the cat in question anyroad..." she said, hauling a reluctant typical tabby cross-breed farm cat out of the cat box that she had placed down on the counter. "Amber. A bit wild around the farm, but fairly easy to handle."

"Right. Just the annual vaccination."

"Aye, that'll do it."

"Any other problems?"

"As normal as anything."

Gill routed out the correct syringe, checking its general health during the awkward silence that ensued, and then vaccinated the cat.

As Sandi stowed the unwilling creature back into the cat box, she began, "So it seems I managed to make a bit of a pig's ear of things last time we properly saw each other."

"Mm? Perhaps neither of us were…" Gill waited.

"You weren't doin' so badly. And I should've thanked you for looking out for me that day. But I was in such a mood, trying to be on my own and have a think. I'm sorry. All I want to say is, I've got some explaining to do. Meet me at the Bull after work? About six thirty should do it."

"I'm sorry. I've been up half the night with a calving at Hillcross."

Sandi looked crestfallen. "Right. Okay…" she began resignedly.

"Just for a bit…" Gill offered.

"Right. See yer later then. Thanks for that." Sandi grasped the offer, cheering up and brooking no further argument nor allowing for a discussion, she walked out abruptly, leaving Gill stranded like a goldfish, her mouth half open, evidently dazed and confused, and, Sandi hoped, perhaps intrigued enough to want to hear her explanation.

CHAPTER TWENTY-EIGHT

Back at The Bull

Gill struggled in through the pub door, fending off the driving rain that was trying to pursue her into the cozier interior. A regular at the bar jeered at her in a friendly fashion, "Right night for a pint!"

She waved vaguely at him and plumped down gratefully into a private high-backed settle near the fireplace, where a cheerful fire was fending off the evening chill.

The Bull was one of the smaller pubs in the village. Dark, with heavy black timbered beams covered in horse brasses and remnants of the past, it was a more private place to meet someone.

She had beaten Sandi to it, but only just. As she wriggled out of her damp jacket, there she was. Sandi appearing through the swinging doors, also drenched, but dressed for it, the rain streaming off her waxed jacket hood. Gill watched her shrug it off, searching the bar and locking eyes with her. She grinned and hurried over.

"Drink?"

"Yes, gin and tonic please."

Sandi dumped her jacket on the coat stand and ordered the drinks.

She brought them over, after a few jovial exchanges with the barmaid. She put the glasses down on the age-worn table, tossing down some packets of peanuts, fell into the settle opposite Gill and stretched her hands out towards the fire.

"There you are." She said in an all-encompassing fashion.

"Here we are…" Gill encouraged.

"Mmm. Yeah. I was getting to that. Foul weather isn't it? The pigs are wading through a foot of mud."

"I was wading through a foot of mud this morning."

"I bet. So…how'r'you?"

"Confused." Gill offered honestly.

"Yeah…me too. The thing is…"

Another customer blew in dramatically through the swing doors, causing some ribald laughter from the regulars at the bar.

"…the thing is," Sandi continued more intimately, leaning forward.

Gill watched her, taking it all in and picking up her glass to drink, hiding behind it.

"…is…well…I'm a wounded animal."

There was a pause, while they both waited for Gill to formulate a suitable response.

She found one. "I'm usually quite good with wounded animals."

"I know."

"So you could, theoretically, be safe in my hands."

"I've noticed. I'm really sorry about the way I behaved…last time. I was getting to be a bit of a mess."

"Yeah, *I* noticed."

"Maybe you only know the half of it, because I've been so stubborn, thinking I can manage everything by myself. Proud, I suppose."

"So what's the other half of it?"

Sandi took a long, thoughtful drink, staring into her glass afterwards, "Well, in trying to control it all, I was losing control of it all. Starting to have panic attacks, if that's what they were."

"But you didn't *say* anything. Symptoms?"

Sandi looked up at her and an affectionate grin crossed her face. "Fast breathing, shaking, racing heart, worst case scenario: feeling faint, weak legs."

"Sounds about right."

"Yeah, that's what the doc said."

"Doc?"

"Years ago in York."

"*Years ago?* Why haven't you said anything sooner?"

"Like I said…proud. So more recently, last week, I saw the local doc."

"Which one?"

"Foley."

"Okay. Decent."

"Yeah. And I've popped a few beta-blockers."

"Propranolol."

"If you like."

"High blood pressure?"

"No. Just to steady things."

"Not too much of that then"—Gill gestured towards the beer—"they don't go well together."

"Yeah, I know. I'm off the whisky…mostly. The thing is…it's the thing with the parents, the car accident the other month, the thought of…losing you."

"Me? And yet, the other day…"

"I know. Why do we do that? Push away the things that matter the most and make it worse?"

Gill paused to consider. "You push away because something's hurting."

"Right…wounded animal. See?" She held out her hand and it was shaking again. "See? That's the effort of talking about it."

Gill felt an immense surge of warmth towards her. Reaching out, she took the trembling hand and sandwiched it between her own. Sandi pulled a sheepish downward smile at her.

They sat there in silence for a moment, savoring the familiar touch and the warmth from the fire. After a while, Sandi's body spoke for itself, her hands calming down.

"Why didn't you say something sooner though?" Gill asked quietly.

"Because *I* hadn't worked it out." She shrugged. "I suppose at first, I didn't want to scare you off by being a trembling dipstick. It was John having one of his brilliant moments, that really threw it into perspective."

"That John. I do love him."

"Me, too."

Again they sat thoughtfully.

"I was having a think about things, too," Gill began, releasing her hands.

Sandi looked at her warily.

"The way I saw it, as I stood at Malham Cove—"

"*Malham*!"

"Great there isn't it? We'll go there together...soon."

Sandi looked elated.

"Anyway, the way I saw it was...here you are on home territory, with all the surrounding history, debris, baggage, or *life* as you may like to call it...and here am I, newcomer, clean slate...well slightly grubby now...but basically I've been allowed to leave my baggage elsewhere for the most part, apart from Inga. It sort of isn't fair really is it? Not exactly an even playing field."

"That's good of you." Sandi looked at her earnestly. "That also makes you the breath of fresh air in the place. My breath of fresh air. And I think I'm afraid that you'll blow away again."

"You should be so lucky...to get rid of me that easily."

Sandi grinned at her. "That's what I spent a bit of time thinking about...get rid? Is that what I wanted? Coz I was doing a pretty good job of shooing you away."

"But I won't always be the breath of fresh air, will I? Stay long enough here and I'll just be another part of the scenery."

"And you think that would be a problem how exactly?"

"Enough. I can't do another moment of soul-searching without some food. Want some fries?"

"Fries? Where does that come from? They're chips around here love."

"Yes. I know. I'll get them." She went to order, leaving Sandi by the fire. Waiting at the bar, she felt the warmth of satisfaction returning to her. The memory of an ice-cold hand clasped at her wrist, a memory that had bothered her from time to time recently, suddenly felt like a burn memory, like the tingling of an old scar, a place where an old injury's pain could still linger. She rubbed it absentmindedly, turning back to look at Sandi, who was staring into the fire in thought, glass in hand. *Choose...* echoed a faint voice at the back of her mind. There were no goose bumps this time. Only an encouraging warmth, a sense of coming home again. *I can choose, I can do that. As long as she can be steadier, as long as it's not going to be a continuous roller coaster.* But the roller coaster had been fun too. She smiled to herself and placed the order. *And Sandi has made herself unwell really... with worry.* She had said 'I think I'm afraid that you'll blow away again.' To someone who had spent most of a lifetime here, Gill was almost ephemeral. But that wasn't her plan. The homely, grounded feel of the place. It made her want to stay. She wandered back, loathe to disturb Sandi, who looked up anyway and patted the settle beside her in a welcoming way.

Gill slid in next to her and Sandi leaned against her shoulder once she had sat down.

"Have you started to forgive me?" she said in a low voice.

"You were forgiven at the wounded animal bit. I get that."

Sandi squeezed her hand between them on the settle.

"I can be a bit thick sometimes."

"Don't say that. We all can be."

"Emotional stuff. It's not always easy or obvious."

"Oh my, that's not just you. Any of us can only try to do a detective job on what's going on. It's not like we're all mind readers. Now telepathy, that would be useful. Some animals seem to have it, sensing danger, reacting to each other's movements."

"I'd like to have the chance to react to your movements again," Sandi murmured.

Gill looked at her quickly and Sandi laughed out loud.

"Let's work on the forgiveness for another hour or so, shall we?"

"I can wait an hour."

"Y'think?" Gill teased. She foraged about for another subject. "How's the building going?"

"Will you come up and take a look? Soon? When you have a moment? To be honest the bottom dropped out of it a bit for me, when, y'know…"

"When you felt it would be best to stop talking to me?" she said it with a twinkle in her eye.

"Er, yes, that."

Sandi stopped for a moment, taking a long pull on her beer. "There's somethin' else I want to ask you." She took in a long breath, as if plucking up courage. "Will you come up to Mum and Dad's grave?"

"Blimey." Gill colored. They hadn't discussed that before. Gill had been told they were buried in the village churchyard, but she had not investigated further. It was hallowed ground. A place where she should not, perhaps, overstep her mark as a foreigner to the neighborhood.

"I want them to meet you…well, kind of…and I have a couple of things I need to clear up with Da…"

"Sure. We should do that." She squeezed Sandi's hand gently in return. "When should we do that?"

"When can you?"

"Tomorrow after the afternoon surgery if you like, if the weather's better."

"It's due to blow over tonight. Let's do that. I'll nip out in the afternoon. What time?"

"Five fifteen?"

"Okay. Thanks."

"I'm touched."

"I'm touched in the head."

"Yeah, I'd started to notice." Gill grinned at her.

They were still smiling when the chips arrived.

After eating, a slight awkwardness hung in the air.

"Sandi, I'm going home now."

Sandi looked at her solemnly. The unspoken implication clear in the statement.

"I'm not trying to make a point. It's just been a helluva day and if it's okay with you, I wouldn't mind digesting everything, the chat and the chips, quietly."

"Yeah, of course." She wriggled out of the settle and stood up, passing Gill her jacket. "Come on, I'll see you home. The car's just along the way."

"I have my car, too."

"Course, the weather. I'll see you out anyway."

"Okay. Let's go."

They zipped their coats, bracing themselves for the outdoors. Sandi waved to the barmaid and held the door for Gill as they left.

It was dark and still pouring with rain.

"I hope it'll blow over tonight," Sandi called above the rain. "Where's yours?"

"Just over the road, car park."

"I see it, me too."

They crossed over the road, fighting the downpour, rain pouring down their jackets. Gill wrestled her keys and turned to say goodbye. Sandi ducked down, pressing a kiss onto her cheek.

"You know how sorry I am."

"Yes, and I am too, especially if I contributed to it. The accident…"

"No need—" Sandi began, but was cut short by Gill pulling her head down towards her and planting a light kiss on her mouth. They looked at each other intently for a moment, lit by the streetlamp, their faces reflective with the rain. Sandi grinned.

"I'm just drained tonight. G'night."

"Sleep well."

A car passed in the road next to the car park, sending a sheet of water splashing close to them. Gill turned and got into her car. She felt she would sleep well. The ghost had perhaps been laid to rest for a while too.

CHAPTER TWENTY-NINE

The graveyard

Gill arrived at the church lych-gate at five fifteen. The weather had cleared overnight, turning into a bracing breeze, the sky a patchwork of blue and scudding clouds. Sandi was sitting on a bench by the church porch, a mysterious long bag dangling from one hand.

They met halfway up the path. Not speaking, Sandi took Gill's hand with a small squeeze and led her around the path towards the rear of the church, then off the path up the grassy hill, between the gravestones.

The turf was damp from the rainfall and Gill was happy to be led along meekly like a lamb, respecting her companion's quiet mood.

She felt honored, knowing how deeply Sandi must be feeling.

Near the top of the hill, Sandi turned to the right, and then Gill could see the plot, near the top corner of the graveyard, where the view was good. There stood a large, single, black granite headstone, its relative newness immediately apparent from the shine, quality and flowers still around it. Clearly, it marked one larger grave.

"We buried them together." Sandi spoke at last, thoughtfully. "So as they wouldn't be alone."

"Hi, Mom, Pa," she continued. "Brought someone important to meet you. This is Gillian. Brilliant new vet at Bridget's."

"Hello." Gill inserted slightly self-consciously into the gap in the surreal speech.

Sandi managed a smirk at her. "Brace yourself Pa, coz I don't want any turning in that grave. Y'know I love you both. Just thought you'd better know, that I love her too and I wish you could've met her properly, but here she is and here am I to introduce ourselves to you in the best way I can think of."

Gill squeezed the hand that still held hers. Just for a moment she seemed to feel watched, feeling the presence of other eyes upon her. She shivered briefly.

"And Pa you ought to know that she's been doin' an incredible job fixing up all the animals, so she's a really useful person to have around and you ought to know how lucky we are to have her here."

Gill made an embarrassed noise in her throat.

"And this is where you can help a bit," she added to Gill, gesturing by holding up the bag.

"We're planting this together."

Sandi pulled a rosebush from the bag, apparently dark red from the buds on it.

"Where shall we put it?" Gill asked.

"I reckon about here." Sandi rummaged in the bag, pulling out a trowel and a plastic bag with some farmyard composted manure. She stuck the trowel in a central vacant spot, between some other plants. "We'll need a fairly big hole."

"Okay." Gill started work. She worked quietly for a while, listening while Sandi chatted about the farm to her parents. It was strangely comforting. She wondered how often she came up here.

After a while, Sandi stopped chatting and took over the digging.

"That should do it. Thanks." She dug the compost into the base of the hole and planted up the rose. "Here, help me bed it in." They finished firming the soil up together.

Sandi sat back on her heels, satisfied. "There. That's joined us to them. It's a marker."

Gill looked and nodded, still awed to be on the inside of such a personal moment.

"When I see that, I'll always know it was you and I who planted it and it was the day I told Dad about you." Sandi packed the remaining pot, the trowel, the compost bag away again into the original bag.

"Yes, we'll always know." Gill offered her hand, assisting in pulling Sandi upright from the ground and into a hug, gratefully received. They stood locked together for a while, heads turned into each other's necks.

Sandi pulled away first, grasping Gill's hands and stepping back as if about to launch into a sidestepping barn dance. "There! That's better!" She looked vulnerable.

"Thanks," Gill said softly, reassuringly. "Thanks for letting me in on that." She thought for a moment. "It would have been nice to meet them."

Sandi released one of Gill's hands and polished the top of the gravestone idly with her thumb. "Well, come on then. Let's go find a coffee and I'll tell you about it." She bent down to retrieve the gardening bag, still holding hands. Gill leaned back and levered her up in a counterbalancing fashion, to which Sandi, once standing again, grinned, and winning the small tug-of-war with her greater size, pulled Gill into an enormous bear hug, ending with the gentlest of kisses on her mouth. Gill felt the ignition of burning flame somewhere in the pit of her stomach, returning the kiss with softness.

"Thanks for being here." Sandi spoke huskily, releasing Gill for a moment, caressing her face across her eyebrow and down one cheek, looking at her intensely. Gill noticed the tear escaping the corner of her left eye and brushed it away for her.

"Shall we get that coffee then?" Gill offered.

Sandi looked at her gratefully, her sheepish grin returning, "Come on then." They grasped each other's hand and Sandi lead them back out of the graveyard.

They crossed over the road, walking back into the village center, Sandi chatting about her parents and her former life.

The coffee shop was still open on the corner of the High Street, so they went in, after cleaning off their boots on the scraper, ordered two lattes and a pastry each, and took a table at the window.

"Mam made fantastic Cornish pasties," Sandi said. "She was able to do them the traditional way, so you could start at one end and it was savory, you know, steak, onion potato finishing up at the other end with apple pie."

"Is that how they go traditionally then?"

"Yeah, somethin' to do with being a snack for the Cornish tin miners. The plaited pastry crust at the top would be where they would hold it with filthy hands, that bit could be thrown away, and the whole thing was a complete meal—two courses."

"What a mine of information you are."

"It would make a great picnic out in the fields at hay making or suchlike. They were bloody hard workers the two of them and real family people, but Dad wouldn't take any nonsense from anyone. I'd get the occasional slap when I was growin' up if I had a dose of the sillies, fightin' with John or somethin' that went a bit too far."

"Probably because you could take John down quite easily if you needed to!"

"Ha! Well, I could in them days anyway."

"People used to do more of it—slapping I mean. My dad left a mark on me once when I was too mouthy to him as a teenager. I suppose it's as normal as being nipped by one of the pack for overstepping the mark or growled at by the alpha male."

"See, I just love it that you see the world through the eyes of animals, too. We're just animals when it comes down to it."

"Just a bit more sophisticated in our expectations."

"Speak for yourself."

Gill laughed out loud, causing the waitress to look up from her tidying up at the counter.

They grinned at each other over their coffees.

Gill sobered up for a moment, remembering something that had been bothering her. "John said you hadn't had a holiday, hadn't taken a break I mean."

"He's probably right. He did mention that."

"He also told me that he would spare you for a break, that you should have a holiday. Do you want to? Shall we bog off somewhere?"

Gill watched for a response. She thought she saw Sandi's breathing rising higher and more tightly in her chest. *Fear of the unknown*...she reminded herself. She ploughed on. "It's just that I'm due for one—Bridget knows—a couple of weeks is possible in July. And I thought...maybe...there's one person in particular it would be nice to share it with...and that would be you, by the way...nothing too grand. Not the car. I've had it with long car journeys at the moment." She rubbed her neck thoughtfully, the remains of the whiplash ache still occasionally reminding her. "I thought maybe coach or train, head down south a bit. You can help to choose too...perhaps see the home of those Cornish pasties, maybe meet my folks as I've come as close as I can to meeting yours..." She let the idea grow for a moment.

Sandi, who had been stirring her coffee and sipping it through this, put down the cup and stretched out the fingers of one hand, as if to see if it was shaking.

After a thoughtful pause she said, "I'd like that. John did say he'd get Frank's best mate in to help over the summer."

"Fantastic. I'll let that thought lie for a while. Have a think about it. See what you fancy and how you fancy doing it. I want to take Charlie, so it would probably have to be the train. I'd hate to shut him up or leave him, particularly as he's so young."

"Charlie. That would be great. Let's finish up. Will you come up to the farm to see how the barn's doing?"

So they paid up and headed back to the farm in Sandi's Land Rover.

Gill pulled up in the familiar yard with some satisfaction. The sense of coming home had been growing in her since Sandi's apology the previous day. It was a rapid turnaround, but she didn't mind, it seemed to be keeping up with the pace of her own healing process with Sandi.

John appeared in a holed jumper and mucky wellingtons from behind the small barn at the sound of the car. He waved, filthy from being with the pigs.

"Hey!" he called as the engine died and they alighted. "Gill!" he added, apparently delighted at the sight of her. He hurried over, but remained at a slight distance.

"I'm not coming any closer, I stink. But it's great to see you!"

They laughed together.

"I'm showin' her the conversion, John."

"Aye, good plan." He grinned from ear to ear. "See you inside in a bit? When I've cleaned up?"

"Of course," Gill replied, feeling the warm glow of the welcome, as John returned to his work.

They followed the sandy track of the heavy machinery towards the old barn at the other end of the yard. The workmen were outside, tidying up for the day after landscaping some of the embankments of soil, evidently working long hours to complete the project.

Sandi called out to them, "Yo!"

"All clear." The foreman waved them through.

"Hard hats still…" Sandi indicated and they both donned the required headwear.

"Here we go." Sandi pushed open the dark-wood, part-glazed front door, revealing the busy interior. "First fix, apparently."

There was a fair amount of noise, drilling in places, plastering in others. Temporary electric lights lit the interior. The staircase was in; rather a beautiful old oak, molded and curving up to the first floor and heavy, newer oak beams blended well with their older colleagues high in the full height atrium in the middle of the space.

"Oh, God. It's beautiful. I mean it's going to be beautiful… it's getting there already."

"I'm glad you think so too. It's not like those millionaire barn conversions down south."

"Er…this is impressive enough, y'know. The fireplace!"

There was a central fireplace, open on two sides, set down a few steps on all sides, like an inglenook, but with a large hood and central chimney acting as a pillar in the middle of the room.

"I know. Amazing, right? It will heat the whole place," Sandi continued, flushing a little with pride. "This side is the main bedroom." She indicated the upper right-hand side of the property. "The opposite side will be a sort of en suite guest room I suppose, not too close, separate stairs too. Come and look at the view."

They walked across to the French doors on the opposite side of what would be the main lounge area to look out to the rear.

"See?"

"Wow!" The view stretched over the first field, which descended rapidly with the opposite side of Blackford visible at the side of the valley and the Winder, ridge and Calf rising beyond. Even the well-worn Winder Path could be seen clearly snaking up the fell side. Kettle's Spout and the mysterious valley beyond were out of sight around the corner of The Calf.

"Winder!"

"I know. Something isn't it? And there's going to be a little terrace and garden." Sandi grasped Gill's hand. "Imagine the sunset from the main bedroom. It looks over the same view. Help me choose the kitchen. I can't decide. I'm torn between Shaker-style olde world and somethin' more sleek and modern. It's going to be fairly open-plan."

They picked their way carefully towards a workbench where the foreman had just stopped perusing some plans and had left to check something or other. Sandi pointed out the layout in relation to the central fireplace, directing Gill's attention to the various areas and angles, bringing to the imagination the life that would take place within the current building-site. Gill veered towards the Shaker-style kitchen, maybe with an old-fashioned dresser built in somewhere too, to keep within the style of the old barn and to match the farmhouse, making it feel familiar and cozy, rather than strange and modern, although loathed to be too influential.

Eventually Sandi took her hand again quietly and looked at her earnestly.

"You said you were good with wounded animals."

"I am an expert you might say."

Sandi smiled. "And that I would be safe in your hands, so to speak."

"That may in fact be the case." Gill was enjoying the formality.

"And I promise you, you'll be safe in mine. You're part of the family. I can't live without you. I can't lose another precious person in my life." Suddenly the formality cracked wide open and the bottled-up emotions of the afternoon started to spill.

"Share this with me. This place. Would you like that?"

Gill dropped the hand held in hers and turned away to look towards the view again. Tears welled up so fast that her vision and the view blurred. A massive sob escaped her. The self-control of the past few weeks suddenly bursting through helplessly.

"Oh bloody hell…" Sandi began quietly, seeming to think she'd mispitched it and rushed it.

Gill turned to her and grasped her into a hug, momentarily unable to speak. *Roller coaster simply didn't describe it.*

More sobs shuddered through her before she could find her voice. Sandi just held her firmly, stroking her back occasionally.

Eventually, Gill pulled away and wiped her face with the back of her hand. "I think…I'd bloody well love to," she managed.

Sandi whooped delightedly and pulled her back into a hug, wiping her face with any spare fabric from her shirt that she could find, tissues or handkerchiefs simply not yet available in the shell of the house-to-be. Finally she pulled her away just enough to raise Gill's smeared face to her by the chin and plant an enormous kiss on her underneath the hard hat.

They had not noticed that the workforce in the near vicinity had paused at the whoop of a woman's voice, downing tools to witness this last bit, so that a sort of comparative quiet had fallen for an instant, broken only by the more distant whirring of a drill and the outdoor heavy machinery.

"Wha-hey!" called a man's voice from above, and a cheer, laughter and some applause broke out around them.

"Gerroff, you daft beggars! Shouldn't you be packin' up to go home?" Sandi yelled at them after pulling away.

The cheers and laughter died down, turning to chatter and back to work noises.

Gill smiled weakly at Sandi, the emotional storm subsiding.

"Come on, let's clean up." Sandi towed her back out of the barn, removing the headgear and back towards the farmhouse. "Sorry about that," she added.

"Don't be. I'm sorry."

"Don't be. You've just made me incredibly happy."

"Me, too." Gill's thoughts were rearranging themselves like a shuffled pack of cards. *Live here?* Live there? In that beautiful place? With this fiery woman? And still be able to do her work? Live with John and Lisa across the farmyard? And Charlie around their ankles? Live in a farm? With animals on her doorstep all the time?

She would have to let Bridget know. Her parents, too. Beyond that, was it really anybody's business other than a change of address card and an invitation to come and stay in the guest wing if applicable? *The guest wing! Sandi!* It was too much. She could feel the tears coming again.

"John?" Sandi called as she kicked open the front door of the farmhouse.

"Yeah?" he called from inside.

"I think we might need a nip of brandy in that coffee."

"I can see...through the window. Come here love."

And he was there too. Embracing them both in a warm, reassuring masculine hug, so that the three of them stood there for a moment in the hallway entrance to the kitchen with arms wrapped around each other. Eventually, Gill wriggled out and ducked into the downstairs bathroom to rearrange herself, leaving the other two to disentangle themselves. They went to charge the coffee with a slug of brandy.

"That went okay then?" she could hear John ask, despite the closed door between them all.

"Okay doesn't cover it." Sandi replied and Gill could see her own reflection flush with embarrassment and pleasure in the bathroom mirror as she eavesdropped, the emotions muddled together. When Gill had recovered herself enough to join them, cozying into Sandi's side on the sofa and wrapping herself around her drink, they were able to set to discussing some possible plans and more urgently, a holiday.

Sandi, Gill noticed through the blur of new ideas and brandy, was neither breathing tightly nor shaking.

CHAPTER THIRTY

The Holiday

Consequently, the farm was busier than usual with heavy vehicles and heavy men trundling around the place, vast quantities of tea being drunk and even more to do than usual. The second fix would begin while Sandi was away.

John had kicked the girls off the site until some real progress was being made. He had almost physically put them on the train to London, as neither of them was much in the mood for driving at all, let alone facing long-distances, since the close call with the car. Gill could feel the comfortable love of a family being knitted around her.

Mel and Inga had long since disappeared back to Norway, for Mel's introductory tour of the region. After weeks of allowing the ankle to heal at Mel's flat, the two of them appeared to have become close. The burdensome weight of association had lightened for all of them, Inga perhaps the least aware of problems resolving themselves with Mel taking off across the North Sea. The two of them had both seemed rather pleased with their developing friendship when Gill and Sandi had visited them for the last time before their departure, much to their mutual sighs of relief.

Now they found themselves on the road. 'An enforced break,' John had said, long overdue for Sandi, adding with a laugh, 'before the honeymoon, farmsitting and Auntie Sandi babysitting.' Sandi wondered if he had anything else he needed to tell her yet. 'Just kidding.' He smirked. 'But I won't rule your services out in future. Circumstances permitting.'

They headed first to London, taking in the sights as well as they could with Charlie, who had been allowed in as the third member of the company, limiting the possibilities a little on a lead in a city: Parliament Square, a boat trip on the river, the great London parks, back street restaurants, and an attempt at a nightclub when they managed to get a sitting service for Charlie.

This was the occasion that Gill had been intrigued about, looking forward to dancing with Sandi in the hot press of people, with the music throbbing through them, the confusion of lights and noise drowning the senses. Occasionally it had bugged her that they had never bumped into each other during her time in York. Or had the chance to feel each other swaying with the music like that. And in a sense it did not disappoint. Sandi fell into easy abandonment with the music, as with the fall of water and the landscape at home, in touch at an instant with the rhythms of instinctive places in her being. They watched each other and held each other appreciatively, Sandi letting her head loll and her eyes half shut to the beat, when she was not nuzzled into Gill's neck.

But perhaps they had outgrown all of these things because it wasn't long before neither of them could bear the general throng of the crowds, where the bustle became jostle and an overdose of stimuli attacked every sense, until they missed the space of the hills, finding themselves heading rapidly out of the city, leapfrogging from monument to town, Stonehenge to Dorchester, washing up eventually by way of public transport at the tiny fishing village of Port Isaac on the North Coast of Cornwall.

"How long do you reckon we can string this out?" Sandi wondered.

"I'm needed back at work next week."

"Yeah, well me too, but we can dream."

So they rented a small cottage just for the week in the middle of the quaint huddle of old fishing cottages in the heart of the village. They had travelled light; afraid of putting nearly healed whiplashed necks from the car accident back out of joint by carrying more than a medium backpack each.

The cottage had everything they needed. Food could be topped up easily: fresh fish directly from the fishmongers' shops at the quayside, bread and pasties hot from the bakeries each morning, other essentials easily found after a steep hike back up the hill to the more modern part of the village.

The house had a view of the cliff-encircled cove and harbor from the tiny upstairs bedroom windows, where a large double bed filled the room almost entirely, old, craggy walls just whitewashed over enhancing the authentic feel of the place. Charlie delighted in chasing the seagulls into the waves several times a day on slow walks to the beach, up the surrounding hills or around the crazy network of miniature streets that made up the lower part of the village, until he was happily tired enough to curl himself at their feet while they lazed away a few hours on the pub terrace looking out over the bay, watching children crab fishing in the rock pools at low tide or the fishing boats coming and going at higher tide, depending upon the time.

Late evenings, once the cheerful pub had closed, were spent wrapped around each other in the bed, the window open to the only occasional sound of a passerby or the settling seagulls until silence descended, the distant waves and faint stir of the sea breeze on the curtains the only company. Waking too early to the tirade of morning gull calls and the stirring of the village, they could lie there, contentedly free of time constraints, although Charlie would eventually need their attention. One of them would oblige him with a walk for the morning paper and a top up of bread and milk, but might return to bed with mugs of tea or coffee made, to see just how long they wanted to stay in bed together.

"See..." Gill murmured at one such point during the week, while she explored the tremors she could create in Sandi. "Travelling with me isn't that scary."

Sandi chuckled. Her eyes half-closed, breathing calming itself. "You're right. I concur. But I do miss the old place. Just knowing how the animals are. Aren't I stupid? Basic?"

"Wild and wonderful," Gill added, smiling at her.

"Actually the worst kind, high maintenance who thinks she's low maintenance."

"Oh my God! *When Harry met Sally*. I love that film."

"Yeah exactly."

"Aren't we all high maintenance, thinking we're low maintenance though?"

"No you're low maintenance thinking you're high maintenance."

Gill mulled this description of herself over for a moment. "You see, I wouldn't say that about myself."

"I rest my case." Sandi rolled them over, so that she was propped on one elbow looking down at Gill pinned gently beneath her. "God. I love you so much it scares me sometimes."

"Don't be. You think I mind? I love you back equally. You are my most favorite wounded animal I have ever treated. I'm not going anywhere."

"Keep treating me, I love it. You're my favorite vet, or should I say doctor."

"Role play...I can go with that...now where does it hurt Ms. Helton? Here...here...let me just take your temperature."

Further words were impossible as Sandi pressed a hard, suddenly urgent kiss upon the mouth speaking the words.

Their most energetic moments had been to climb the coastal path above the town to Port Quinn—Charlie back at the cottage this time—to join a kayaking group exploring the sea caves in the cliff-enclosed bay and, on another day, a typically daring escapade by Sandi who had spontaneously decided to brace herself for the jellyfish, swimming from neighboring Port Gaverne around the headland to Port Isaac. Gill had stood breathlessly nervous with Charlie snuffling anxiously, until the progress of a familiar bobbing head could be seen through the decidedly choppy waves.

"When did you get that good at swimming?" Gill had asked later.

"Well, as you know, I'm pretty decent in the local pools and streams. But at college, I was often dragged out at six a.m. to do thirty lengths before the day started."

"Really?"

"Well, it was easier than being on milking duty."

On the return trip to Yorkshire they dropped in for one day at Gill's parents' house, where Sandi received tremendous praise for her easy attention to a newly arrived sow housed at the bottom of the garden. Thankfully her parents were relaxed and liberal enough to let the girls have the spare double room for the night, saving them all from any awkwardness of embarrassment.

CHAPTER THIRTY-ONE

Home

The big day had been set for the first Saturday in August. Being traditionalist enough to want to do it the right way and please everyone as well as themselves, John and Lisa had booked the church service at St Mark's in the village, 'so that Mam and Dad can watch it all happen' John had added ruefully, and a reception at the Golf and Country Club.

Sandi felt fortified for the event now she and Gill were more secure. The barn conversion was nearly complete. The workmen were just tinkering at the guest room end inside and finishing the landscaping, the driveway down to the road, so that Gill and Sandi would not have to approach through the farmyard every time they arrived or exited. The kitchen and bathroom were complete and it was time for them to move in.

Suddenly they felt like schoolgirls again, leaving home, packing and unpacking for a holiday or university. That childish rush of excitement surged through them to put belongings where they would be most effective and loved. "Like having a doll's house...on a giant scale," Gill had noted.

"You had a doll's house?"

"For a while."

"Funny, I hadn't seen you as having a doll's house. It's kinda cute!" Sandi pinched her playfully as she passed by carrying some bed linen.

Gill had given notice on the mill cottage rental and was ready to move out with a confident glow, remembering the encounters that had established where they were today. But when she heard from the letting agent that the owners were selling, she put a smart offer in for the place and snapped it up before it even went on the open market. She felt attached to the memories and the security of knowing it was there. Only a tiny bit of her was unromantic enough to think of it as a bolt-hole if Sandi's moods were worse than she had imagined. It would make a great holiday let, too, and she would have the perfect excuse to revisit it to tidy, decorate, watch the mill race, have coffee at the craft café and keep the connection. Sandi loved the idea, too. To her, it was Gill putting down roots in the village.

They had spent time shopping for furniture in the antiques shops, in Blackford and further afield. At an antiques warehouse, really a converted mill building, on the edge of the Lake District, they had routed out the right size of antique pine dresser for the gap in the kitchen; a matching worn, loved and still beautiful kitchen table and set of chairs; a curved wooden settle for beside the fireplace; and a smaller, straight one for removing boots, just inside the front door; some copper saucepans which were still in good condition; and an antique Tiffany lamp that threw a range of colors from its stained-glass shade. In Kendal, they had bought cutlery and crockery, ordered a corner sofa and matching armchair in a warm red pattern and made plans for the guest room. They had headed home with a happy hole burned into their pockets, although Sandi insisted hers was the lion's share, as much of this had been budgeted for by her and John in the first place. She and John jointly owned everything at Helton. Complicated rewritings of wills would have to wait for now, Sandi added slightly cryptically, which Gill chose to read as wondering how they would rejig everything for Lisa's part in the arrangement. Sandi said a prenuptial agreement had been put in place already to protect everyone. And if anyone else became part of it, at which point she squeezed Gill's hand, it would all have to be readdressed and rebalanced again.

The enormity of the concept was such that it was best left unacknowledged for now. It was enough to take one step at a time, the two of them living in the moment of planning this first major step together. Sandi's bed and bedroom furniture were being moved over from the farmhouse. In the mill craft shop, they had both loved a large watercolor of 'Winder and The Calf on a Summer Evening' and Gill had bought it as her housewarming gift to the house. It was going on the living room wall, away from any possible effects of heat from the fire.

And finally it was complete. There had been a few nightmares along the way, such as the rock bed that made it difficult to sink the sewer pipe to join the mains sewer at the farmhouse junction, and a misjudgment in one of the picture window measurements, but now it stood beautifully, humbly at the far end of the farm buildings, privately away from the farmhouse. The old stones had been carefully preserved and recycled to clad the outer walls, the timber roof supports had been buttressed and strengthened, reclaimed slates tiled the roof. Inside, beyond the roomy porch, with a long stone seat where muddy boots could be shed, was breathtakingly spacious, clean-lined with granite work-topped kitchen, open-planned around a reclaimed inglenook fireplace with steps down to it like a miniature amphitheater, perfect to perch on with friends and a glass of wine to thaw the winter chills of the hilltops. Some expense had gone into draft-proofing and heat economizing, with triple glazed windows on the sides of the atrium that faced the prevailing wind. The master bedroom was dark in color, warm and welcoming, commanded by Sandi's familiar, generously accommodating bed inviting further adventure. Guest accommodation was set as far away as politely possible, in the upstairs galleried annex set into the opposite end of the barn.

They were ready to mark its completion with a group of their closest friends and favorite colleagues. Gill's parents had made the journey up from down south to join the wedding party and be the first honored guests in the annex. It was fitting that they could squeeze in a small drinks party, before the main event.

Once the oohs and ahs of admiration had died down, canapes had been dispatched and early departures had been made by some, 'to save themselves for the big one' the remaining stoics sat around the fireplace, where a small fire danced even on this early summer's evening as the sun set over the hills. Charlie was stretched out in front of it, still recovering from the excitement of a long walk earlier in the day and the new house, so filled with interesting people and new smells.

"Reckon Mum and Da' would've been proud of us," John commented sleepily, turning a tumbler of orange juice around in his hand. He was keeping his head clear.

"Yup, reckon so," Sandi murmured. "The place has turned out well." She was staring into the flames, her head on Gill's lap.

"And maybe they wouldn'a have the guts to do this, the way you have," Bridget's husband, Alan pointed out. Bridget was resting her head comfortably on his shoulder. "They were more old school than you two."

"Alan…" Bridget began.

"Nah, it's all right Bridge, he's gotta point. Thanks, Al."

"I like the way you've made these cushions fit the fireplace steps. Really comfortable." Bridget veered the conversation away a little.

"That was Gill's doing," Sandi added.

"She got that skill from her mother," Gill's Dad, Graham, pointed out. He had collapsed into the nearest armchair, cradling a small whisky in one hand. Gill's mother, Mary, was lying, her feet stretched out, on the sofa.

"I would have liked to have met them," she said quietly.

"And me," Gill added.

"Yeah." There were a few murmurs of assent and a small, friendly silence fell on the company.

"Well, I don't know about anyone else," Mary pointed out, "but, I'm going to have to go up in a minute, if I'm not to look like a wreck in the wedding photos tomorrow."

"Ha!" John exclaimed. "Me, too." And he made to stand up, creakily for effect.

"Now, now, you're not that done in!" Gill smirked. "We want you skipping back down that aisle tomorrow."

"Yeah, Lisa's probably well down the path of her beauty sleep by now," Sandi added.

John grinned. "I bet. It won't be hard to skip tomorrow, I can tell you."

"I want to see it." Becka giggled. "C'mon!" She pulled Andrew to his feet. "You're on driving duty, remember?"

"How could I forget?" He gave his charming smile. "But tomorrow is another story…"

The departing group returned their glasses to the kitchen area and Sandi hauled herself off Gill's lap. The pair of them went to the door to see everyone out and assist with coats. Graham and Mary called a friendly 'Good night to all!' and disappeared up the opposite staircase to the guest room.

"See yer tomorrow, Sis!" John grabbed his sister by the shoulders and kissed her on both cheeks.

"Sure you're all right in the farmhouse?" she asked quietly.

"Absolutely fine. Last night of freedom, before Lisa henpecks me into submission. Nah! I'm only jokin'. But I might have the dogs up on the bed for company."

"Yeah, you might not be allowed to do that in future!"

"We'll see…anyway best man's knocking on the door at six tomorrow morning."

"Off you go then. We're here if you need us."

"Yeah, that's nice, isn't it? Just across the yard from each other."

"Yeah. Love yah…"

"Love yah, too."

"Love yah three…" Gill added as she gave him a huge hug and kiss.

And suddenly, the door was closed and all was quiet, apart from a little soft jazz.

"And there y'go, it's all ours." Sandi put her arm around Gill and nuzzled her neck.

"Wow. I'm still pinching myself."

"Come and pinch me."

"Kitchen first."

"Okay Miss…"

The sun was still setting over the hills, the sky a dark pink, as they packed the last glasses into the dishwasher. They stood for a while at the patio doors, breathing in the fresh air of the night as darkness drew in, while Charlie did his last tour of the garden.

"So Bridget's definitely not at the surgery tomorrow?"

"She'll be there in the morning, beforehand. Then she's leaving Nathan and a locum to hold it during the service. Then Nathan's coming to the reception and the locum will call them if anything urgent comes in."

"Great, I have you for two whole nights and a day sandwiched in between."

"And what a day!"

"Yeah! Thank God I have you to get me through it. I'm going to bawl like a baby."

"You'll be fine. And yeah, I'm there. I'm here."

"Yeah, I know." She drew the doors closed and locked them. "Let's go up."

"Gladly." Gill whistled for Charlie and allowed herself to be led by the hand. "I am soooo ready for bed. That went well. It was really lovely to have them here."

"Yeah, I think it's been baptized, blessed, wetted as they say."

"And we can continue the ceremony, upstairs…"

"I was hoping you might say that. Great, isn't it, that visitors are far away down the other end?"

"Let's hope sound doesn't travel down the eaves of the roof."

"D'ya think? Naw…you're having me on."

Gill let her hand linger on the polished oak of the curved bannister as they followed the stairs upwards, Charlie's claws clicking on the wood. I must clip them…So graceful and beautiful, she thought as she looked back down over the living space, thinking herself again so fortunate and blessed too.

Their bedroom was separated from the staircase by a small upstairs hallway, with a bookshelf and a chest of drawers. Fortuitously, two doors soundproofed this area to the rest of the house. Charlie went obediently to his basket in the corner of the room, although they both knew he would be squeezed in somewhere on the bed by the time they woke in the morning.

After a moment in the bathroom, Gill went round to her side of the bed and allowed her clothes to fall carelessly to the floor in a heap, to be dealt with in the morning. She felt so tired, but contented. She stepped out of the pile and clambered naked into the crisp sheets, watching Sandi take a little more time, emerging from the bathroom next door after a while and undress herself, folding and hanging her clothes up with more deliberation.

Such a well-brought-up girl, she thought and then felt a stab of sadness and empathy for her, that those who had brought her up would not be there for them tomorrow, even though her own parents were here now, in this house, if a little greying these days. She was suddenly very clear on how Sandi was feeling—both happy and lonely—sad for her parents and her brother's wedding day without them there. The years without them...the years of struggle and forging onwards.

"Come here," she said softly, pulling back the cover on Sandi's side. And as her partner, her lover, climbed in, she pulled her over and wrapped her up in her arms, as if the love, warmth and companionship from her could help to soothe the past. And they both lay there. Warm skin on warm skin. Warming a space within the cool sheets. Knowing that tonight no more was needed than the comfort of this still, undemanding touch in each other's company. Lying there in their own space, a slice of moonlight cutting across the room from a chink in the curtains. Falling gradually, contentedly asleep, as those sorrows of the past gave themselves up in the haze of the dreams of the night, even though they may yet return in the morning, particularly that morning, as they inevitably did every morning.

CHAPTER THIRTY-TWO

Wedding day

In the morning, Sandi rolled affectionately over to Gill, having been separated from her by the night's tossing and turning and woken by the nuzzle of a cool, wet nose as Charlie hoped for the day's action to commence. Kissing her fondly, her eyes wet from disturbed dreams, she whispered, "I love being with you. You make me stronger today."

Gill rolled towards her, folding an arm and a leg over her, waking only gradually.

"What's the time?"

"About seven thirty."

"Then…" she ran her fingers down Sandi's face. Feeling the remains of the tears, she propped herself up on one elbow and stared at her, puzzled. "You okay?"

"Mum and Da should've been here today."

Not knowing how to find comfort in words, she kissed her tenderly, brushing away the damp with her fingertips. Sandi's answering kiss was fiery, firm in its return, fueled by gratitude, loneliness, emptiness, grief, love, too confusing a mixture to rationalize or explain.

"Do we have time?" Gill managed as she gasped for a breath.

"Not really. Come to the shower?"

"Come in the shower at this rate."

"Let's do it."

"Get yourself in there. I'll just let Charlie out into the garden."

And that was how Gill decided she could help Sandi fortify herself for the day. Taking the mud-free route to the farmhouse with her parents and Sandi, after a light breakfast, to see John in the smartest suit and tie she had ever seen him in. This Sandi would find easier to do, Gill imagined, because the memories still held for them of shower water running down their bodies that morning, and of how she had held on to Gillian fiercely, apologizing to her for her ferocity.

They drank coffee together, with a tiny nip of brandy in it for courage, in the farmhouse kitchen, for the last time with the current status quo, while Frank Harris ran all the dogs around the large meadow for them. He had promised to sit up at the farm during the service, to be there for security and reassurance, and vaguely the feeling that their parents' spirits would have company if they came there seeking it. He would join them later at the Country Club.

"You look handsome," Gill said, planting a kiss on John's cheek and smoothing his collar over his cheerful tie. He grinned at her and gave her a bear hug. Steve, best man, childhood friend, clapped him on the back.

"How's the speech going?" Sandi grinned at him.

He pulled a piece of paper from a pocket and fingered it nervously.

"A work of art." He winked.

"And the rings?" Gill added.

Steve pretended to have lost them and then revealed them from his top pocket like a magician.

Gill looked across the table at Sandi, dressed immaculately in a trouser suit and open-necked lilac shirt. Her heart spilled over with pride and sympathy, all at once. She looked down into her own lap, running her hands over her tight skirt, while her high-heeled shoes toed Sandi's beneath the table, trying to avoid scuffing the careful shine on both.

Sandi caught her eye and smiled wryly. Memories of gasping for air and avoiding mouthfuls of shower water crossed between them. Of being arched into each other so hard, that if Sandi had let go, both of them would have collapsed onto the tiled floor in a heap. She trapped Gill's foot between both of hers and squeezed.

Gill's mother sat at the top of the table, feathers in her pale blue hat dancing as she cut chunks of fruit cake for everyone, because 'everyone is going to need their strength later', apparently doing her best to contribute to the deep fondness in the room. Her father cracked a few 'you should have seen us on our wedding day' stories, that did the job of keeping the mood in the right place, until Steve went to bring the especially highly polished black Range Rover around to the front of the house. This would be their wedding car today. Suitable in all senses.

All six of them piled in, after John closed the farmhouse door, patting it lightly with the words, "All change!" meaning the end of the line, beginning of a new journey.

At the church, spilling over with flowers, friends and family from near and far, there were many hugs and greetings to give and receive. Only when they had settled in the front right pew did Sandi release the clasp she had on Gill's hand, instead wrapping her right ankle around Gill's. Even here in the church, their thoughts seemed to be strengthened by the memories of them on their knees on the hard tiled floor, hot water pouring down their hair and shoulders, Sandi gasping quietly for mercy 'for the love of whichever God or Goddess of love is performing this torture'. Gill's kiss turning to a smile.

They had gone weak-kneed to the bedroom to dry each other's hair and recover normality, before presenting themselves in all their finery, still a little flushed, for breakfast in the kitchen.

Gill took Sandi's hand again, squeezing it gently. She turned to look back down the church, catching the eye of familiar faces: Becka, Andrew, Bridget, Alan, farmers, wives, children she knew only a little, smiling.

"It's buzzing." She leant into Sandi.

"I know."

"It's worth a look back."

Sandi, who had seemed to be focusing in a rigid way upon the nave of the church, turned to look at the chatter and excited smiles of anticipation, everyone waiting for the bride, the action to begin. John was wandering up the aisle with Steve, having a quick word with some and shaking hands with others. And suddenly Gill saw that she was grinning. As if aware of life moving forward in the right way. She sighed and her shoulders fell by inches.

"Oh, my. What a sight!"

"Right!"

Eventually, John reached the front pew, falling into it in mock relief, putting an arm around Sandi and giving her a massive squeeze.

"Mind me hair," she teased.

"As if!" He laughed and ruffled it purposefully.

"Jeez." She shoved him hard, playfully.

"Don't hospitalize me today."

"Hah!" She sized him up. "Y'know you look bloody gorgeous. Anyone would think you were getting married or something."

"Nobody told you?"

And suddenly, a hush fell on the congregation; a moment's pause while the congregation rustled to its feet, John and Steve took up their positions, until the organist struck up "Jesu Joy".

Gill, Sandi and Steve looked back, grinning at the sight of Lisa on her father's arm, veiled and so beautiful. John remained stoically forward, waiting a while, before succumbing to the temptation to look. And then the look on his face, awe, pride, delight, to Sandi it appeared to be worth so much. Gill's father winked at them both as they looked back and the joy of the occasion surged through them. Gill could feel Sandi relaxing, the realization sinking in that nothing much was expected of her today, just to enjoy herself. Nobody had petitioned her for a speech, perhaps sensitive to her feelings on such an emotional day. The most she would have to do would be to lift a few chairs, chat, laugh at the jokes and dance. Her voice lifted with strength, surprising Gill in the first hymn "For All the Saints". Lisa's family had taken so much of the responsibility off their shoulders. The reception, flowers, cake, gifts, bridesmaids, invitations, everything had been scooped up happily into their planning. It had just fallen to John to whisk his bride off for the honeymoon. And he had enjoyed sifting through options with Sandi, fastening eventually on Burgh Island for two nights and a week in Jersey, because they could take a look at the milk farming practices there somewhere among the trips to the beach, and that would not be too long to be away. Lisa was understanding about these things. She knew she was marrying the farm as well as John, and anyway, farming was in her bloodline too.

Somewhere in amongst the 'I dos', John and Lisa's evident pleasure, the signing of the register and the recession down the aisle, Sandi seemed to realize everything was going to be just fine.

"John and Lisa! It's how it should be for them," she whispered to Gill.

The photographs outside the church, on a bright and slightly breezy summer day, caught the genuine smiles of warmth from them all, the relaxed laughter as they tried to tame hats, hairstyles and Lisa's floating veil in the typically temperamental Yorkshire air.

Gill had left her car in the village overnight, so she drove her parents and Sandi on to the country club. Two shire horses and passenger carts had been loaned by Meadow Farm, into which bridesmaids, Lisa's family and many other guests hauled themselves, to the accompaniment of the romantic clop of impatient hooves. Others walked or drove themselves. Steve was on his way to the club already, chauffeuring the newlyweds in the Range Rover.

"If Mam and Da are having a float around today, there'd be plenty to see!" Sandi pointed out, watching the tourists take photos of the carts as they pulled away from the church lane.

By the time the carts reached the club, John and Lisa were lined up to greet everyone and as guests were shepherded in by the staff to shake hands, hug, choose their drink and start to peruse table plans, piles of gifts and the spectacle of crystal glasses and candelabras, the warmth and bonhomie was spilling over.

Everything had been arranged perfectly: perfectly specially, perfectly friendly, perfectly warmly. Although evidently a cut above everyone's usual social engagements, requiring the pinpointing of clothes that didn't usually need to see the light of day in a normal week in Blackford, it was real and homely. The children had been allowed the use of the outdoor pool, and on this warm-enough day to use it, parents took their glasses to poolside tables, while their little ruffians who had behaved themselves for long enough at the church service ran off some steam, flinging themselves into the pool, the teenagers bouncing off the springboard, a couple of toddlers sitting in the paddling pool playing with plastic balls and ships. Anybody who knew what it was like to have children knew that this was a moment of genius in the planning from Lisa's family, at least if you wanted the children to sit quietly and enjoy their meal. With a lifeguard on duty, waiters passing around trays of light nibbles, champagne and other delights, it was a moment to feel free and relax before the formality of the meal and speeches and to pace oneself for the next round. Even Steve and Lisa emerged into the sunshine, chatting and grinning, working their way around all their friends and family. Lisa had done something ingenious to her outfit after the first meet-and-greet, so that the veil, train and part of the length of the dress had been shed, leaving her shapely legs on display up to the knee with pretty white kitten heeled shoes and a relaxed look for her too.

Sandi and Gill had already had massive hugs from the pair of them, happy tears springing to Sandi's eyes as she looked at them so closely. Now they were on the far side of the pool, in a part-shady spot, Sandi kicking back and relaxing in the sunshine pacing herself on a half pint of beer, Gill's parents sheltering in the shade sipping at a bubbling glass, Gill close enough to Sandi to hold her hand loosely between the arms of their chairs. The screams of the children meant not an awful lot of conversation could be had, or if it was, then parts of it would inevitably have to be repeated.

"What a glorious day!" Graham pointed out, raising his glass to the hills in the distance, simmering in the sun, outlining the brilliant blue, cloudless sky.

Sandi had closed her eyes in worship of the rare warmth of the sun. Gill sat chatting on and off with her parents, a grateful moment of relaxation. Sandi seemed at one with everything, Gill noted, and if her head was buzzing with the social and familial gear-change that weddings bring, at least in the way that her own head was buzzing with the speed that everything had been happening to her this past year, she wasn't showing any signs of stress about it. No tremors. No shakes. Sandi grinned, still with her eyes shut, as if reading Gill's thoughts. Gill squeezed her hand lightly as she chatted to her dad. Sandi opened her eyes, briefly, winked at her and closed them again. All was well. Suddenly her social conscience seemed to pinch at her and she hauled herself to her feet, taking her glass.

"Thanks again for comin'," she announced suddenly, addressing Gill's parents. "I'd better go and chat to aunts, uncles and cousins," she added, a little reluctantly. "Join me in a minute?" she asked Gill.

"Sure, the meal can't be long now…"

She sauntered away. Mary smiled, as she watched her daughter watching the departing figure.

"She's doing all right with it all, isn't she?" Mary offered.

"Not bad at all!" Gill meant this on several different layers to herself. "Well, I suppose I should go and chat to Bridget and some of the others, before we all have our sit-down." And with that she levered herself up. "You two will be okay?"

"Fine, we've already met and spoken to more people than you realize! Lisa's family is so friendly."

And it wasn't long until the bell rang, and children were being hauled out of the water, hastily toweled and re-dressed in a slightly more relaxed version of their finery, perhaps a best T-shirt, rather than a best dress, to go and choose between scampi and chips, shepherd's pie or pick from the adult buffet, which was a splendid affair, ranging from hot to cold, an Elysium of different dishes from which to choose.

It gradually became evident that no formal seating plan was in action, and although the table layout had been mapped, seating was not prearranged. A certain modern fluidity was in evidence that meant guests could circulate and change places if they wanted to between visits to the buffet tables, the table service tidying discreetly behind them when necessary, making the whole affair tremendously sociable and not in the least clipped by forced formality, children swinging their legs beneath their chairs and tucking into chips dipped in ketchup, if they were not enticed by the many more sophisticated dishes, ranging through harissa chicken to blue cheese and sun-dried tomato soufflés, with myriads of sides.

The afternoon was punctuated with amicable moments: Ethan appearing from standing guard at Redbridge's and being handed an orange juice with a teasing cheer; Frank Harris arriving from Helton and his sons greeting him with a fresh pint, another cheer; a rollicking, but thankfully brief, best man's speech; gifts for the bridesmaids and Lisa's best friend Emma; thanks to all in a concise and polite way; cheers each time John and Lisa were caught snatching a kiss with each other.

A friendly dismissal from the master of ceremonies meant that children were free to attack the pool again, guests could wander to the bar or the coffee lounge, or their rooms if they had splashed out for them, while tables were cleared and stowed and the reception room would be gradually rearranged and transformed into the evening's disco. John, Lisa and many guests seem to evaporate, to their rooms or to find a corner somewhere. A few appeared to be finding time for nine holes of golf or a quick game of tennis before the evening's entertainment. Frank Harris's eldest son of three had gone up to watch Helton Farm. Sandi made checks on the situation chatting to Frank, but it was a good day with no emergencies at the farm. The gods or spirits were looking down kindly upon them all. Bridget had returned to the veterinary surgery, relieving Ethan.

Gill had overseen her parents settling down for a rest with the newspapers in the voluminous armchairs of what had once been the smoking lounge, when Sandi intercepted her.

"Come with me," she commanded mysteriously, leading her through the ladies' changing rooms to one of the back porch exits out to the golf course.

There she indicated their hiking boots tucked under the wooden bench.

"I'm glad you didn't notice I'd pinched them. Dropped them off here yesterday."

"Really? You fancy a hike?"

"Nothin' much goin' on here for a few hours. Y'know me. Can't bear to be cooped up for too long. I reckon we can make it to Winder and catch the six twenty bus back to make it for supper and dancing."

"Dressed like this?"

Sandi pulled a locker key from her pocket and waved it at her. "It's all planned…jeans, jumper, backpack…I've only had a pint and a half. Your folks know."

"They do? It's a conspiracy. Oh, why the hell not? That's a great idea."

It seemed odd walking away from the wedding ceremony. Odd too without Charlie snuffling in and out of the bushes. But also a refreshing step back into normality. A first journey experiencing the 'after' of John and Lisa's new coupledom. Within half an hour they had managed to change and had climbed partway up the hillside, the celebrations and screams of children muted now as the breeze encircled them. The sun was warm on their faces, making only T-shirts necessary at this stage.

"I wonder what John's up to?"

"Maybe don't think too hard about it."

Sandi guffawed at the thought. "Good plan."

As they threaded their way through a copse of trees on the lower slope, Sandi paused for breath, leaning against a relatively young tree, looking back towards the view. Gill caught her breath; then leant into her for a hug.

"Think we'll need a shower when we get back down."

"Won't be like this morning's."

"Hah!"

They pressed on up the hillside, hardly talking, enjoying being away from the social gathering, the expectations of amusing small talk. The breeze became fresher, the more sultry valley air further below them now.

"I didn't expect this," Gill said, looking down as the valley began to reveal itself as a map.

"I know, right? Full of surprises me."

"Uh-huh! That I've noticed. The farm will be easy enough to manage without John?"

"Now that's what he worried about too! Frank and sons are up for the whole of their trip, aren't they?"

"Yeah. That's a relief."

"And then, when they're back, well…it will be getting used to the new status quo. I'm kinda startin' to look forward to that."

Gill hugged her round the shoulder with one free arm, the other caught at her own waist, pinching a stitch brought on by eating heavily then walking hard. She grinned at her. "Me, too. Come on, we have to make it to the top."

"Coming, boss." And they struck out for the top of the ridge.

CHAPTER THIRTY-THREE

Winder has the last word

When they had climbed together past Winder and along the ridge to Kettle's Spout, they sat on one of the larger boulders at the top in the late afternoon sun.

Sandi broke their mutual silence. "Close your eyes, listen…"

Gill, glad to oblige Sandi when she was in one of her more emotive moods, did so. Immediately, with the visual beauty of the scenery removed, their ears became even more finely attuned to the distant singing roar of the water, the call of a skylark, the distant hum of a light aircraft, the breeze stirring the air.

"Hear that?"

"What in particular?" Gill murmured.

"The voice?"

Gill listened harder, a more conscious effort.

"Don't try too hard, let the sound of the waterfall wash over you…"

Gill tried again, smiling at the faint lunacy of the request. Gradually, as she tried to hear it, the water started to sing like a distant sigh of a woman, changing, breathing heavily then lightly.

"You know the legend…"

"Uh-huh…do you think she's really out there?" Gill asked.

"I like to think so. I like to think of all the people we have lost being 'out there' looking down kindly upon us," Sandi said softly, coming closer to Gill's ear and kissing it lightly, soundlessly, with soft lips.

Gill shuddered and opened her eyes. "I like it when you talk like that. It's like you're joined to the soul of the earth around us."

"I am." Sandi smiled. "Didn't you know that?" She looked more serious. "Sorry…for last time we were here."

"Mmm."

"It was crap of me." She placed an apologetic kiss on Gill's forehead. "So what, if Pa didn't have his head fully around it all. How many people are still stuck in the Dark Ages? You're right, we are the bearers of life for that maiden who lost her life. Perhaps she was one of my forebears. We might be linked in the family tree. What do you think? Do you think she would really have wanted the power of choice that we have? To have the lives that we can lead?"

"Yes. I like that thought. I don't like it that she couldn't have that right to choose. And still there are people out there today who might not have that right, who are terrified of being made to do something else or unable to speak up for themselves, like she was."

"Somewhere in her way, she and her kind started the journey that we make today."

"She's singing forever. Or maybe it's a myth of violent weather the wind screams no, or breathes yes in a softer breeze. A place to come, they say, when a decision has to be made. But who knows?"

"Until the waterfall dries up."

"It never does though?"

"Never in history. So on it goes."

"So does she for all eternity. That's a reminder for us and anyone else who cares to listen." Sandi put an arm around Gill and pulled her in closer.

"Lucky us then."

"Mmm. It would be nice if we learned from history. If the world learned from these stories."

"And yet we make the same bleedin' mistakes."

"We *have* learned though. From each other. From the context of the legend."

"Yeah *we* have."

"Let's be an example, shall we?"

"Yeah. I'm for that. Live life the way she would have had it if they had only listened and been freethinking enough to understand her and believe in her."

"Precisely. Let's do that."

"We'll make it for the bus if we head down now. Dancing awaits."

"I've been wanting to dance with you again…"

The faint memory of an icy grip on Gill's wrist drifted away on the summer breeze as they set out for the descent. *Choose…* it had said. Gillian had made her choice and here they were, silhouetted together as clearly as the rocks on the Winder Path.

And the waterfall sighed with pleasure.

Bella Books, Inc.

Women. Books. Even Better Together.

P.O. Box 10543
Tallahassee, FL 32302

Phone: 800-729-4992
www.bellabooks.com